"I'll find you a ride, Alexis," Dawson said quickly. There was no point in antagonizing her any more than she was already antagonized, not with everything else that was going on.

Alexis eyed Dawson and smoothed some hair behind her ear. "And would you, by any chance, be riding in this car?"

"Sure. Excuse me. I'll be right back." Dawson took off, looking for Emily LaPaz. He knew Emily had her own car and had arrived separately from her mom. So, unless she'd gone to the hospital, maybe Emily could drive them back.

Suddenly, the full weight of the predicament hit him. He was now the sole proprietor of Potter's B and B extension, Dawson's Inn. And he had absolutely no idea what he was doing.

Dawson's Creek™

Running on Empty

Based on the television series "Dawson's Creek"™
created by Kevin Williamson

Written by C. J. Anders

BOOKS

First published 2000 by Pocket Books a division of
Simon & Schuster Inc., 1230 Avenue of the Americas,
New York, NY 10020

This edition published 2001 by Channel 4 Books
an imprint of Macmillan Publishers Ltd
25 Eccleston Place, London SW1W 9NF
Basingstoke and Oxford

www.macmillan.com

Associated companies throughout the world

ISBN 0 7522 1952 9

9 8 7 6 5 4 3 2

A CIP catalogue record for this book is available from
the British Library.

Printed by Mackays of Chatham PLC, Chatham, Kent

For Julius and Trinity

Running on Empty

Chapter 1

"Okay. I admit it. I hate the book," Joey Potter told Pacey Witter as they headed across the school parking lot toward his truck.

"Potter, don't you know it's illegal, not to mention un-American, to hate *Moby Dick?*" Pacey asked, as he threw his books into the truck.

Joey scowled and leaned against the truck. "This macho Melville man-against-nature thing really gets on my nerves. Why are we celebrating literary hormones run amok? And why did he have to make it a whale?"

Pacey fake-punched her bicep. "Celebrating is beside the point, Potter. Big test on Monday is more relevant."

She threw him a baleful look. For some reason he was really irritating her today. "I liked you better when you were allergic to studying."

He wagged a finger at her. "An untruth."

Joey sighed. "Why couldn't we just have a normal test with questions that we can memorize one day and forget the next? But no, we have to do a dramatic team presentation that explores Melville's allegories and metaphors. It scares me to think what Ahab's peg leg might mean."

"Hey, remember our Lit teacher told us he worked summers on a fishing boat during college? Which was, might I remind you, in the late sixties? And notice how he kind of zones out every now and then? My theory is, he did just a little too much acid back in the good ol' days," Pacey opined. "Flashbacks."

"Thank you, Captain Ahab."

"Hey, guys," Andie McPhee called, as she headed toward them, her arms laden with books. "I am beyond prepared for this study session. I've got four excellent books of commentary and criticism on *Moby Dick.*"

"Gee, I was thinking more along the lines of *Cliff's Notes,*" Pacey remarked.

"Fortunately, I know you're kidding," Andie told him. "Oh, Jack told me to tell you he can't make it—something about helping to set up for the firehouse dinner tomorrow night."

Pacey nodded. "Ah yes, the annual Weekend of the Whales is upon us once again. Our sleepy seaside village is about to be overrun by tourists with binoculars Superglued to their eyebrows, searching for a glimpse of Free Willy."

"At least it's good for business," Joey said. "Potter's

Bed and Breakfast is booked solid for the weekend. I just wish it wasn't a weekend when I had so much homework."

"Hey," Dawson Leery said, as he joined them. "Sorry I'm late. I got cornered by Emily LaPaz. She wants me to video her parents' anniversary party next week."

"Did you say yes?" Joey asked, as they got into the truck.

"For a hundred dollars, I definitely said yes." Dawson jumped into the flatbed of the truck, as did Andie. Then Pacey cranked the oldies station up—he loved to listen to oldies, much to the irritation of his friends. With the windows rolled down, the air filled with the sounds of Jefferson Airplane as he pulled the truck out of the parking lot. Joey knew it would be pointless to try and talk to him over the music, so she turned to stare out the window.

It was nice of her friends to agree to study at her house, Joey thought. Normally, her house was the last place she wanted to study, let alone have a study session with her friends. For one thing, her house was on the proverbial wrong side of the tracks—or, in her case, wrong wide of the creek. For another, her sister Bessie's son, Alexander, was going through his "no" stage—his answer to everything was "no," followed by hysterical screaming. It tended to put a damper on the concentration factor.

But Bessie had her hands full trying to get ready for all the guests who would be arriving at the bed and breakfast for Whale Weekend, especially since they'd significantly raised their prices and were offering a full American plan, meaning three meals a day. Bodie, Bessie's significant other, had left Capeside that morning on a family emergency, and he was the resident chef. His departure had left Bessie and Joey frazzled before the weekend even began, because now Joey would have to watch her screaming nephew and study simultaneously. Keen.

She glanced over at Pacey. He was bellowing along with Grace Slick. She turned back to the window. Maybe she did know why she felt irritated by Pacey; she was confused about their relationship. They had both been Dawson's two best friends forever, but their relationship with each other had always been pretty much as sparring partners. Now, things had changed. She and Dawson were no longer a couple. Andie and Pacey were no longer a couple. And she and Pacey were . . .

Well, that was the problem. She didn't know what they were. She didn't even know if she *wanted* to know. She did know, however, that she definitely didn't want whatever it was they were—or weren't—to hurt Dawson. That would be a pain too intense to imagine.

Not that she was prepared to admit that to anyone but herself.

Twenty minutes later, when they all piled into Joey's kitchen, they found a note from Bessie on the table telling them she'd decided to leave early to go food shopping and that Alexander was with her. She'd also left them a platter of homemade cookies on the counter. "It was nice of her to make cookies for us," Andie said, reaching for one.

"Believe me, it's even nicer that she took Alexander with her," Joey said. "Let's work in the dining room."

Pacey popped a cookie into his mouth and grabbed the platter, Dawson took the milk out of the fridge, and Joey and Andie got the glasses. Then they settled down around the dining room table.

"Okay," Andie began, making a bridge out of her fingers. "I'm assuming we've all finished reading the novel?"

"Assume away, McPhee," Pacey replied.

"Excellent." She pulled a stack of three-by-five cards from the pocket of her notebook. "I've taken the liberty of making a few notes that might jumpstart our creative process. What does the whale represent? What does the quest for the whale represent? What does the color white represent? What does Queequeg represent? And why does the narrator want us to call him Ishmael?"

"I know how you adore running the academic show, McPhee," Pacey said, "but I offer a counter suggestion."

She smiled. "I'm all ears."

Pacey pulled a video from his backpack. "One copy of *Moby Dick,* starring Gregory Peck as Captain Ahab."

"Peck is great," Dawson said, "but other than that, it's over-the-top melodrama cloaked in a title that people know and a story that everyone is familiar with."

"Well, I've never seen it and I think it would help," Joey said. "Right now my mental pictures of this novel are highly lacking in creativity. All I can picture is the wide ocean, a whaling boat with an overdose of testosterone powering it, a poor whale they all want to kill, and a Nantucket sleighride to nowhere."

"All in favor of watching the flick?" Pacey raised his hand, as did Joey. "A tie. It's a shame Jen's in another group on this project. Because she definitely would have gone for the movie."

Joey pulled a quarter out of her pocket. "Call it in the air," she told Dawson, and flipped it.

"Heads."

Joey caught the quarter neatly into her palm. "Tails. Let's go to the videotape." Without hesitating for a moment, she led the way to the living room.

"All right, but I don't see how watching a movie is going to do anything except waste time," Andie said grumpily. "We're getting tested on the book, not the film." She settled down on the couch next to Pacey. Dawson sprawled on the carpet. Just as Joey was sticking the video into the VCR, she heard the unmistakable screams of baby Alexander. She winced.

"Joey?" Bessie called from the kitchen, barely audible over her son's wailing.

"Here," Joey called back, without much enthusiasm.

Bessie appeared in the doorway, a screaming Alexander on her hip. She took in the group. "My lucky day. My car is full of groceries and my son needs his diaper changed. Which would you guys like to help with?"

Joey, Dawson, and Pacey quickly headed out the kitchen door to help bring in the groceries. Bessie simply laid Alexander on the kitchen table and attacked his diaper bag.

"Is that sanitary?" Andie asked tentatively, making a face. Alexander stank.

"He's not writing his name with it on the walls, I'm just changing his diaper. Anyway, it's nothing that a gallon of bleach can't take care of." Bessie smiled at her son. "Yes, my little man," she cooed. "You miss your daddy, don't you?"

"Want the perishables in the fridge?" Pacey asked, appearing in the doorway with grocery bags in both arms.

"Yeah, thanks," Bessie replied, holding the baby down with one arm and fumbling in the bag with the other. "You guys are a lifesaver. Did Joey tell you we're fully booked for the weekend?"

"She did," Dawson replied, as he placed two bags of fruit on the counter. "I think it's great." He headed back outside for more bags.

"Canned goods in this cupboard, right?" Pacey asked.

"Yeah." Bessie finished changing Alexander, thrust him into Andie's arms, and then wiped down the table with bleach. "Happy?" she asked Andie, who was holding the baby very gingerly.

"Deliriously, thank you."

Dawson, Joey, and Pacey appeared in the doorway again, holding even more groceries. "That's it, Bessie," Dawson said. "You have enough food here to feed a small army."

"Hey, I really appreciate your help," Bessie told them. "I know you guys came over to study. I can take it from here."

"You sure?" Joey asked, taking in the chaotic scene in the kitchen, and instantly feeling guilty over her impatience with her sister and her nephew.

When your mom is dead and your dad's in prison, it kind of helps to stay close to the only family you still have, she thought.

"Positive," Bessie replied. "What are you studying?"

"Moby Dick," Andie said.

"Ugh. Better you than me. Can't they pick something a little more environmentally conscious?"

"Yeah, they should." Joey smiled at her sister and kissed her nephew. "By the way, thanks for the cookies, Bessie."

"You're welcome."

The group headed back into the living room. They had barely settled down again by the VCR when Alexander began to cry at the top of his lungs.

"I'm thinking future opera star," Pacey said. "That kid has quite the set of lungs."

"And he uses them with ever-increasing frequency," Joey muttered, reaching for the VCR remote to bump up the sound. Maybe trying to study at her house hadn't been such a good idea after all.

The phone rang. Bessie yelled, "Joey, can you—"

"I got it," Joey yelled as she headed for the phone. "Potter's Bed and Breakfast." It still felt weird to her to answer her own phone that way, but they couldn't yet afford a separate line for the bed and breakfast. *Maybe after this weekend's bookings,* she thought.

"Hi, Potter's? This is Freddie Sumo. I'm just calling to confirm our reservation for tomorrow."

Joey opened the reservation book that sat by the phone and flipped the pages until she came to tomorrow's reservations. "Yes, Mr. Sumo. We've got you down for two double rooms."

"Great, great. There are two beds in both rooms, right?"

"Yes, sir."

"Great. Would you say the beds are well reinforced?"

Joey had no idea how to respond to that, so she went for, "Pardon me?"

"Sturdy, is what I meant," Mr. Sumo clarified.

"Yes, I'm sure the beds are all sturdy, Mr. Sumo," Joey assured him. "We'll see you and your party tomorrow, then. Good-bye."

As she hung up the phone, she could see her friends looking at her with quizzical expressions.

" 'The beds are all sturdy, Mr. Sumo'?" Pacey echoed. "What was that all about? On second thought, maybe it's more than I want to know."

"He asked me if the beds are reinforced," Joey explained. "I answered him. In this business, the customer is always right."

"We're definitely talkin' honeymoon or weekend-away-cheatin'-on-the-wife," Pacey guessed.

"You are such a cynic," Andie chided him. "What if the man simply has a bad back?"

"Or if he just happens to still be passionately in

love with his wife of many years with whom he still has vigorous and creative sex three or four times every night?" Dawson asked.

He and Pacey exchanged looks. "Nah," they both said at the same time.

Thankfully, Alexander abruptly stopped screaming. Joey checked her watch. "Let's fast-forward through the trailers and get to the movie. I've got at least two hours of homework to do tonight on top of this project, and I have to help Bessie bake for the weekend. Our brochure promises homemade baked goods for breakfast every morning."

"I can help, if you like," Andie offered. "I love to bake."

Joey smiled at her gratefully. "I might just take you up on that."

They hadn't gotten more than five minutes into the film when they heard Bessie cry out, followed by a loud crash. Without hesitation, they ran into the kitchen to see what had happened, fearful that she had somehow dropped the baby.

But it wasn't Alexander. He was sitting in his high chair. As for Bessie, she lay writhing on the floor, a gallon of pistachio ice cream nearby.

"Are you okay?" Joey asked, going to her sister.

"I am such an idiot," Bessie fumed. "I was rushing to get the ice cream into the freezer and some of it had dripped on the floor and boom, I slipped." There were tears in her eyes, which was alarming. Bessie never cried. Joey didn't know if they were tears from feeling overwhelmed or if her sister was actually hurt.

Andie put the ice cream into the freezer and got a sponge to wipe up the floor, while Dawson knelt down next to Bessie. "What hurts?" he asked her gently.

"I kind of landed on this ankle," Bessie said, cocking her head toward her right ankle, which was already swelling up. "It did one of those turn-to-the-side things."

"That looks nasty, Bessie," Pacey said.

Dawson nodded. "I think we need to get you to the emergency room."

"Like I have time for that," Bessie snorted. "Who's going to get the place ready for the weekend?"

"But Bessie, you have to—" Joey began.

"I'm sure I just bruised it," Bessie insisted. "I can walk it off. Can you guys help me up?" Dawson and Pacey carefully helped Bessie to her feet. Foot, actually, because she was holding her right foot off the floor. They supported her on either side.

"You think you can try and put some weight on it?" Dawson asked.

Lips pressed in a thin, white line, Bessie gingerly put some weight on her right foot. And cursed loudly.

Bessie never, ever cursed in front of Alexander.

"That's it, we're going to the hospital," Joey decided. Her sister didn't argue.

"Theoretically, this is coffee, although the vending machine looked like something from the first act of *Peggy Sue Got Married*." Dawson gingerly held the steaming Styrofoam cup out to Joey.

"No thanks." She managed a weary smile.

"Can I get you anything to eat?" Andie asked, rocking Alexander in her arms. Thankfully, he'd been sleeping the whole time the doctors were checking out Bessie.

Joey shook her head. "Want me to take the baby?"

"I love holding him," Andie insisted. "It makes me glad not to have one."

"Listen, we've already been here almost two hours," Joey pointed out to her friends. "I appreciate your support, but it's beginning to be overwhelmed by my guilt. I know you all have to study and—"

"You know we're not leaving you, Potter, so why go into your little song and dance?" Pacey asked.

Joey closed her eyes and let her head loll back against the wall. She was too tired to spar with him right now. After they'd brought Bessie to the hospital, they'd had to wait nearly an hour before a fresh-faced redheaded nurse brought them to an examining room. By that time Bessie's ankle looked like a purple baseball.

After another half-hour, the same nurse came out to tell them Bessie was going up to X-ray. They'd been waiting nearly another hour since then. It was nearly seven o'clock.

"Miss Potter?" Joey opened her eyes. The red-headed nurse was standing before her.

Joey jumped up. "Is my sister—?"

"She'll be done in a minute," the nurse said. "Her ankle isn't broken."

"Oh, that's great!" Joey exclaimed.

"It's badly sprained, though," the nurse continued.

"So she needs to stay off of it completely for three or four days. She'll have a printed list of instructions, ice, heat, and so on. We'll give her a pain prescription, too."

Joey nodded.

"It really is important that she stay off of it," the nurse emphasized. "Bad sprains can cause more long-term problems than breaks if they aren't properly treated."

"I won't let her walk, I promise," Joey assured her.

The nurse nodded. "Well, she'll be out in just a few minutes. She's signing some forms now. Thanks for bringing her in."

When the nurse left, Joey sagged back into the ugly orange plastic chair. "We have an inn full of people showing up tomorrow," she said, sounding dazed. "No Bodie, Bessie can't walk, just me and an infant—"

"Melodrama does not suit you, Potter," Pacey chided her. "You think your nearest and semi-dearest will let you down in your hour of need?"

"You know we'll help you, Joey," Dawson added, draping an arm around her and giving her a quick hug.

"You're not alone," Andie added.

Joey thankfully looked around at her friends' faces, and she really did know she could count on them. It made all the difference in the world.

As the nurse wheeled Bessie out, her right ankle heavily bandaged, crutches across her lap, Alexander woke up and immediately began to bawl. "I'll take him," Bessie said, holding out her arms. She cuddled her son but he only yelled more loudly.

"He's hungry," Bessie said.

"I fed him," Joey told her.

"Well, he's hungry again." She gave Joey a wan smile. "I am so sorry to put you through this, Joe."

"No problem," Joey assured her valiantly. "I'll just go pick up the scrip for you."

Bessie tapped her pocketbook. "Got it already, thanks, Joe. Dawson, could you reach into the side of the baby bag and get a jar of food for him? Then let's get him home."

Joey nodded. The sooner she got Bessie home and settled, the sooner she could plan exactly how she was going to make it through the weekend with a houseful of paying guests, who all expected three excellent home-cooked meals a day. Plus a sister who couldn't walk. Plus a screaming baby.

Yes, her friends volunteered to help her. It was a good thing. She was going to need all the help she could get.

Chapter 2

"Joey, can you bring me the reservations book?" Bessie called.

Joey took one more quick peek in the oven—she had made three giant lasagnas according to a recipe that Bodie had faxed over that morning. So far, so good. They seemed to be cooking evenly, and the mechanical timer atop the stove still showed seven minutes of baking time left.

"Coming, Bessie!" Joey shouted upstairs. She closed the oven door, grabbed the black book from the kitchen table that held reservation information for the B and B, and brought it up to Bessie's bedroom. Her sister was ensconced on her bed, her injured right ankle elevated on a pile of three pillows with ice packed around it. Joey looked at the ankle—the purple color had deepened. Before she'd gone to bed, Bessie had talked confidently about being able to wrap it the next day and get around on crutches. But there was obviously no way she'd be able to do even that.

Bessie motioned for Joey to give her the book—she was deep in conversation with someone on the phone. "Uh-huh," Bess said distractedly, as she quickly flipped pages in the book, looking for something. "Here it is. Mr. and Mrs. Roland Martino, from New York. It says here you're coming for your twentieth anniversary, which is really lovely, but without a credit card you can't have expected us to—"

Joey could hear an excited male voice coming through the phone, though she couldn't hear what he was saying. Now Bessie held the phone away from her ear—Mr. Martino was screaming. Whatever was going on was not good.

"Yes, Mr. Martino," Bessie said, her voice even. "I do understand. And we will honor your reservation. See you this evening for dinner." With a groan, she clicked off the portable phone and dropped it on the bed next to her.

"Problems?" Joey asked, trying to keep her voice low, because Alexander was sleeping on a blanket on the floor not far from her feet.

"Big ones," Bessie confirmed. "That was Mr. Martino from New York. He and his wife booked for Whale Weekend three months ago. No guarantee, no credit card, nada. Never heard from them again. Thought they wouldn't show up. Which is why I rented their room to the honeymoon couple from

Maine. Patrick and Candace Ackerly. They're going to be in Room Three."

"At the risk of pointing out the obvious, you can't rent out a room you've already rented," Joey said.

"Wanna bet?"

"Bessie, this is crazy. Why didn't you just tell Mr. and Mrs. Martino that their room was no longer available?"

"Because Mr. Martino is a journalist and he happened to mention that he's a close personal friend of Fred Fricke, the travel writer. How close I won't be asking."

Joey gulped. Fricke was the writer who had come and reviewed the B and B last year. He had a lot of clout. It would not do at all to irritate him by turning away his close personal friends.

"And that's not all," Bessie went on. "The Ackerly guy called a little while ago and informed me that they're bringing a videographer with them to videotape their honeymoon."

"Where are we supposed to put a videographer?"

"In my room, if necessary," Bessie replied. "Ackerly said he'd pay double for the room since they didn't give us notice before. Evidently it's a last-minute wedding present from the bride's rich parents."

Joey sat on the edge of Bessie's bed. She felt sick to her stomach. "This is impossible."

"Yep."

"How could you double-book rooms, Bessie? What are we going to do?"

"I don't know, Joey, but I'll tell you what we're not going to do. Turn away customers. You know what we're getting a head this weekend? We could pay our mortgage for half a year if they all show up."

"But we've only got three rooms here. And we've got the Sumo brothers in two of them, and the Martinos, and the Ackerlys and their photographer—"

"Videographer—"

"Whatever. What I want to know is, where are we going to put all these people?" Alexander made a noise in his sleep and turned over. Joey held her breath—the last thing she needed was for him to wake up now.

"We are two intelligent women, we can figure this out," Bessie said calmly.

"Great," Joey replied. "I'll just let intelligent you take the lead. And forget renting out this bedroom. You're not supposed to be up on that ankle. You can't be up on that ankle even if you wanted to, and I need to know where you'll be at all times, so you're staying put."

Bessie smiled ruefully. "It gets worse."

Joey gave her a baleful look. "How so?"

"Well, there's this oceanographer, Dr. White, and her twin grandsons. I spoke with her the day before yesterday. She insisted that she'd held their rooms with a credit card when she booked a few weeks back—"

"But she didn't," Joey surmised.

"Bodie took the reservation and he's not here for me to ask. Anyway, she confirmed this morning."

"Let me guess—you told her yes, too."

"Of course I told her yes. I figure one old lady and

two little boys could share this room and I could sleep on a cot in your room."

"Bessie, your room has a private bath, which is kind of important for a woman who can't walk. You aren't giving up your room."

"Fine. We'll set up tents for 'em on the front lawn, then," Bessie snapped. She winced and settled her injured ankle at a different angle. Joey knew her sister was in pain. She didn't want to take the pain medication because it made her woozy and she wanted to be alert to care for Alexander.

She closed her eyes, rubbed her temples and took stock of the situation. They had more guests than they could handle for the weekend. Way more. The guests were going to arrive in about six hours, all expecting a wonderful Whale Weekend.

But they only had beds for some of them.

How could they possibly avert the impending disaster? There had to be something . . .

A burning smell wafted upstairs from the kitchen. Bessie sniffed the air. "Joe, do you smell—"

"The lasagna!" Joey bolted from the room.

"Think of something!" Bessie called after her. "We've got to figure out what to do."

Joey ran into the smoky kitchen and pulled the scorched lasagna from the oven, just as the fire detectors went off. Alexander must have heard them upstairs, because he began to howl.

"Swell. Just swell." Joey dumped the former lasagna into the sink, turned on the faucet, and watched the charred mess steam.

Figure out what to do my foot, she thought. *You*

figure it out, Bessie. I, for one, am planning to just run away from home. I'm sure the Martinos have a lovely place in New York. And I happen to know it's going to be empty.

"Hey, Joey, what brings you around?" Gale Leery looked up from the vat of coleslaw that she was literally stirring with a canoe paddle. "I don't suppose you showed up to help me stir this stuff?"

"Sure, why not." Joey took the canoe paddle and swirled it into the humungous container of salad. All around the kitchen of Gale's restaurant there were enormous containers of food for the annual firehouse fried chicken dinner, an all-you-can-eat Capeside tradition that always kicked off Whale Weekend.

Gale kissed her cheek. "Thanks, sweetie. You just freed me to go get more shredded carrots."

"Hey, Joey." Dawson popped up from under a counter. He had huge Tupperware containers in both hands, which he set on the counter. "Just have an urge to indulge in oversized culinary pursuits?"

"Oh, you know me, nothing but time on my hands," Joey said breezily, as she forced the paddle through the thick salad mixture. She made a face. "Doing this could put a person off coleslaw for life."

Dawson took the paddle from her and took over. "Why so depressed?"

"Who says I'm depressed?"

"If I can't read your face after all these years, Joey, I must be going blind."

Joey sighed and leaned against the counter. She

didn't know what to say. And she sure didn't know how to ask Dawson and his parents what she needed to ask them. Gale bustled back over to them and poured a huge bowl of shredded carrots into the vat. "This must be what it's like to feed an army."

"Dawson told me about your sister," Mrs. Leery said. "That's a bad break. If there's anything that we can do to help, just let us know."

Joey managed a wan smile. The last thing in the world she wanted to do was to ask Gale to help get her and Bessie out of their mess, but . . . "Mrs. Leery, please don't say that unless you mean it," she finally said.

Gale stopped what she was doing. "You haven't called me 'Mrs. Leery' in ages, Joey, so this must be serious."

"It is. I could use some help in figuring out how to avert an impending disaster."

Gale wiped her hands on a dishtowel. "Go on."

"What's up, Joe?" Dawson asked, clearly concerned.

"Here's the situation. We've massively overbooked the B and B for the weekend. How is a long story and why is because, frankly, we need the money to pay the mortgage."

Gale nodded and waited for Joey to continue.

"It gets worse," Joey warned. "We're on full American plan for the weekend, meaning three allegedly delightful meals a day."

"And Bodie's away," Dawson realized. "Bessie can't walk. And cooking is far from your long suit, Joey."

"Thank you for confirming my insecurity in that area, Dawson," Joey told him.

Gale tapped a finger against her lips. "How many extra people are coming?"

"A lot," Joey said, too embarrassed to mention the actual number.

"I'll give you two rooms," Mrs. Leery declared. "Mitch and I will do cots in the basement. Dawson, you'll give up your room, won't you?"

Dawson bowed playfully. "Your need is my command, Joey."

"I can't ask you two to do that—" Joey began.

Gale held up her hand to silence Joey. "You didn't ask. I offered. And I know you won't deprive me of the opportunity to help a friend."

Joey smiled. "All I can say then is, 'thank you.' "

"You're more than welcome." Gale hugged her.

"Does that take care of all your overbookings?" Dawson asked.

"I think it still leaves us one short, believe it or not," Joey admitted.

Gale looked thoughtful. "You know, when Dawson was little, Jen's grandmother's washer and dryer both went on the fritz when she had a houseful of company. Mitch and I did laundry for a week for her. I bet I can call in a favor—"

"I can't let you do that," Joey said quickly. "I mean, it's incredibly generous of you, but—"

"But it's the best solution to your problem," Gale filled in. "It's already done."

"Consider this an across-the-creek extension of Potter's B and B," Dawson suggested. "It's so unique, you should charge them extra."

"This is no big deal, Joey," Gale said.

Joey smiled ruefully. "Frankly, we all know it's quite a big deal. And I appreciate it more than I can possibly tell you both."

"This is what friends are for, sweetie," Gale told her warmly. "Besides, a little rearranging, a little cooking, we'll meet some new people, it'll be fun."

Dawson grinned at Joey. "That's my mom," he said proudly. "Just out of curiosity, Joey, who gets my room?"

Joey pulled a file card from her pocket. "You will be the hosts of newlyweds from Maine, Patrick and Candace. They're on their honeymoon. According to Bessie, he's nice, she's rich."

"Well, we won't need to worry about feeding them," Gale said. "When Mitch and I were on our honeymoon, we never came out of the hotel room."

Dawson winced. "More than I needed to know, Mom."

"You'll only need to handle coffee and toast or something," Joey added quickly, "and only if they're really early risers. We'll feed them a real breakfast, lunch and dinner over at our place."

"You're cooking for all these people?" Gale Leery asked doubtfully.

"Sure," Joey replied, hoping she sounded more confident than she felt. "Oh, one other thing about the newlyweds. They're bringing a videographer with them to record their every bill and coo." She glanced at her card again. "Her name is Alexis Wesley. More than that, I don't know."

"Well, the newlyweds should definitely get the

master suite and the videographer will get your room, Dawson."

"Sure. Just one thing, though, Joey. How will we know when it's time for meals at your place?"

"Pacey's taking care of that," Joey assured him. "He's putting up a big dinner bell in the backyard as we speak. People will hear it in Boston."

Dawson felt hurt, momentarily. If Pacey was putting up a dinner bell, that meant that Joey had already talked to him about the crisis at the B and B. And that meant that Joey had talked to Pacey about it before she had talked to Dawson. It was logical, in a way, considering the current state of their relationship. But once upon a time, Joey would have come directly to him; do not pass Go, do not collect two hundred dollars.

Well, now was not the time to think about that. It was too confusing. And painful. And he didn't have any answers. Better to concentrate on the crisis at hand. And try to help Joey in a way that Pacey hadn't.

He looked at his mom. "Do you absolutely need me here for the next half-hour, or can my kitchen sentence be commuted long enough for me to run an errand?"

"It's not indentured servitude, Dawson," Gale replied. "What's up?"

"I'm going next door with Joey so she can ask Jen's grandmother to join the moveable feast."

"I think I'll have better luck," Gale said. "Just get me the phone." She dialed Jen's grandmother. When she answered, Gale quickly filled her in on the situation.

". . . well, that's incredibly generous of you," Gale said, giving Joey and Dawson a big thumbs-up sign. "Joey or Bessie will be in touch with you soon."

She hung up and grinned at Joey. "Done. Potter's B and B now has two branch offices."

". . . and Whale Weekend kicks off with the annual firehouse fried chicken dinner at the Capeside firehouse," Joey told Mr. and Mrs. Martino, who were only half-paying attention to her, already unpacking their belongings in Room One. "If you'd like to go, we have directions from the B and B. It's very easy to get there."

She waited expectantly for either of them to glance up from their unpacking. Neither did. "Or you could just let me know later," Joey added lamely.

Finally the couple exchanged looks, then Mr. Martino looked at Joey. "My wife doesn't eat anything that ever had a face."

"Oh," Joey replied slowly. "Well, she can dig right into that delicious coleslaw, then."

Mrs. Martino shook her head frantically. Joey was beginning to wonder if the woman actually had the ability to speak.

"My wife doesn't eat mayonnaise," he explained. "Too much saturated fat. I, however, am always interested in an all-you-can-eat meal. I try to make up for what she doesn't eat whenever possible. It is all you can eat, isn't it?"

"I think so," Joey replied.

Mrs. Martino gave her husband a meaningful look. He looked at Joey again. "Since we're on the

American plan, do you think you could come up with something for my wife instead? Soup, maybe? Vegetable is good, just please make sure not to use beef or chicken stock. Also, she prefers organic vegetables."

Mrs. Martino nodded emphatically.

"But—" Joey began.

"We booked on the American plan, and that includes all three meals," Mr. Martino reminded her. "And you won't be feeding me dinner. So the vegetable soup for my wife is no problem, I'm assuming?"

"No problem at all," Joey assured him sweetly. In her mind, she was already prying open a can of Campbell's which she could disguise with a few slices of fresh carrots and some frozen mixed vegetables. She and Bessie had planned that their guests' first meal would be at the firehouse. But then, they hadn't planned on anything like the Martinos.

"That will be all," Mrs. Martino said dismissively.

So she could speak after all, Joey thought. To issue orders to the scullery maid, anyway.

"Just a moment," her husband added, looking around. "Where did I put my wallet?"

"It's over there," Joey said, cocking her head toward the chair, where he'd draped it. "But I don't need a tip, sir."

"Nonsense, I insist."

As Joey waited, Mrs. Martino pulled out her cell phone and punched in some numbers, then she began a spirited conversation with someone about some kiddie cartoon show with "dehumanizing values." Joey vaguely recalled her mentioning that she had a marketing job for some children's television production company in New York.

"Really, Shelly, that show is utterly demeaning to women, and I for one want to see it off the air," Mrs. Martino insisted into the phone.

Mr. Martino slapped a single dollar into Joey's palm. "There you go, young lady. Thanks."

Joey felt like flinging the dollar in his face, but she pocketed it. "If there's anything either of you need, please don't hesitate to let us know." *Not that you will,* Joey added in her mind.

Mr. Martino had already turned away as if Joey had already left. And Mrs. Martino was now personally berating the person at the other end of the phone line.

Joey slipped out of their room. She headed downstairs, where Dawson and Jen were waiting for the rest of the guests to arrive. Pacey was in the backyard, fixing the hammock.

Moo-o-o-o-o!

Joey stood stock-still on the stairs. Something outside had just mooed. As in cow. As in really loud cow.

Moo-o-o-o-o!

There it was again, sounding not unlike a heifer in heat. "What on earth is that?" she called, hurrying to her friends. Jen and Dawson were staring out the front door.

"You're not going to believe this," Jen said. "Look."

Joey peered out. There were two enormous sport utility vehicles parked in the front driveway. One of them was bright red; the other had been painted black and white in the pattern of a cow. To continue the cow motif, actual steer horns had been lashed to the hood.

Moo-o-o-o-! The animal husbandry-themed SUV had an animal-husbandry-themed horn.

Now, two of the most enormous men Joey had ever seen got out of the cow on wheels. Two others, equally huge, stood by the red SUV. They were beyond huge, actually. Gargantuan. Gigunda. Not one of them could have weighed less than three hundred and fifty pounds, and the biggest one had to go a good four hundred plus. And none of them were smaller than six-foot-five.

"It looks like the defensive line of the New England Patriots," Dawson muttered. "No wonder they asked about the beds being sturdy."

"Sumo Brothers," Joey mused. "Do you think they're professional Sumo wrestlers? They're not even Japanese!"

The biggest of the four was the first to see Joey and her friends in the doorway. He gave them a friendly wave. "Hi!" he shouted. "We're the Fabulous Flying Sumo Brothers. Great to be here, man!"

Joey waved back.

"Whoa," Pacey uttered. "Joey, I hope you plan to make a lot of pancakes tomorrow."

"Well, let's not just stand here, Dawson," Jen nudged him with her elbow. "We're supposed to be helping."

"Right," Dawson agreed. "Let's help them with their bags. Not that they look like they need any help."

By the time the threesome reached the Sumos, they were already taking their bags out of their SUVs.

"I'm Joey Potter." She held her hand out to the biggest guy. He shook it, his hand roughly four times as large as hers. "Welcome to Potter's B and B. We want to do everything we can to make your visit pleasant."

"Hello Joey, I'm Fred Malamala, better known as Freddie Sumo," he said, grinning hugely. "From Maui, which is heaven on earth. Ever been?"

"Can't say that I have."

"You need to get there one day, you'll see what I mean."

Joey quickly introduced Dawson and Jen.

"Any of you speak Japanese?" Fred asked.

"Gee, no," Joey replied, confused.

"Neither do we," Fred said, laughing heartily. "It's a joke, man. You know, we call ourselves the Fabulous Flying Sumo Brothers because we're all so big."

"I see," Joey said, though she was pretty sure she didn't really see at all.

"We aren't Sumo wrestlers or even WWF wrestlers. Just oversized American slam poets, bringing words of beauty to the masses. Guys, come meet our hosts!" The other three guys dropped their bags and trotted over.

"Joey, Jen, Dawson, the Sumo Bros, Ike, Mike and Elvis," Fred introduced them. Then, Joey introduced her friends. She couldn't help noticing that Elvis kept eyeing her like she was his favorite dessert. He had an Elvis hairdo, complete with swept-back hair and long black sideburns.

"So, you said you're slam poets?" Dawson asked.

"The four biggest poets in North America," Fred said proudly. "That's combined weight, not fame. At least not yet."

"Pardon my all-too-ignorant ignorance," Pacey said, "but just what is a 'slam poet'?"

"It's sorta like rap, you know, rhyming lyrics about stuff people care about, but without stealing anyone's music to go behind the words," Ike explained.

"Beatniks started doing it in the fifties," Mike added. "You know, in coffeehouses. Way cool."

"We have kind of a unique spin on it," Fred said. "Tag-team slam. It's awesome."

Elvis pointed at Joey. "You're pretty awesome yourself, pretty mama."

Pacey scratched his chin. "So, just a wild guess here, but you're an Elvis impersonator, right?"

Elvis eyed Joey. "Long story. I could whisper it in your ear later on, if you like."

"Gee, I'll be really . . . busy later on," Joey managed.

"I may be sorry I asked this," Jen began slowly, "but how did the four of you meet?"

"We met at a weight-lifting event," Fred said, "like three years ago and found out we were all poets. So two years ago we started this group. We perform at coffeehouses, on college campuses—but our fave is elementary schools. We get to show the kids you don't have to be a skinny geek to love the written and spoken word. We call ourselves the Sumos for fun."

"But we don't wear the diapers Sumos wear onstage or anything," Ike added.

"Good to know," Jen said, managing to keep a straight face.

"So, we've been on a tour of schools in the northeast," Fred told them. "And my man Elvis is from Wisconsin. He's never seen the ocean, much less a whale, so we decided to come to Capeside. Should be big fun—and that ain't no fat joke."

"We're happy to have you," Joey said. "We'll just carry your bags in."

She reached for a huge bag but Elvis got to it first. He picked it up with one hand and picked Joey up in the other. "Which one to deliver to my room?" he joked.

"Put me down," Joey said through clenched teeth. "Now."

"Sorry, pretty mama." Elvis set Joey down. "I was just funnin' with you."

Joey clenched her jaw so that she wouldn't tell Elvis exactly what she thought of his "funnin." She managed a tight smile. "No more lifting of the innkeeper. After you." Joey gestured toward the front door. The other Sumos took their own luggage and followed Elvis.

When they got into the house, Joey moved in front of them, leading the way. Elvis caught up with her. "Hope I didn't go too far out there."

"You did, a little," Joey said.

"We cool with each other now?"

Joey nodded as she opened the door to his room.

"There's a luggage rack right over there for your suitcase."

"Thanks." Elvis set it down. "So, maybe you and I can hook up later. Go for a spin in the moo-mobile. I got a killer CD system in there. And mattresses in the back."

Someone snorted a laugh in the doorway. It was Jen, who clearly had overheard Elvis's proposal. "Now there's an offer you can't refuse," she told Joey, trying to keep a straight face.

Joey blushed. "Look, Elvis, I don't want to be rude, but I am not looking for any kind of personal involvement."

Elvis nodded. "Whatever floats your boat, babe."

"Good. Just so we understand each other." She opened the door to the bathroom. "You'll find extra towels under the sink, if you need them."

"Wanna come by later and scrub my back?" Elvis asked, leering at her.

Joey felt like screaming. "Didn't I just tell you that I am not interested in a personal involvement?"

Elvis shrugged. "It doesn't have to be personal."

Fred came in and threw his suitcase on one of the beds. "Elvis, you hittin' on this nice young lady already?"

"I made her an offer she can't refuse," he smirked.

Jen cracked up. Joey decided to ignore Elvis completely. Arguing with him was clearly futile. She headed for the door. "If either of you need anything, don't hesitate to let me know."

"You know what I need!" Elvis called as Joey shut the door.

Joey leaned against the wall and groaned. "Lustful Elvis is all I need."

Jen did her best Elvis impression, curling her lip. "You're irresistible, pretty mama."

"So not helpful." They headed for the front hall. "One more come-on from Mr. Graceland and the innkeeper hat comes off and the boxing gloves go on."

Chapter 3

"What comes to mind is: 'yowza,' " Pacey exclaimed, as he looked at the overloaded boat. From bow to stern, the boat was filled with video equipment, luggage, sporting goods, and not-yet-unwrapped wedding presents. "These people didn't get married to each other. They got married to an upscale shopping mall."

Dawson nodded and rubbed his arms to warm up. The day had turned cold and cloudy, and rain threatened. "Kind of gives new meaning to the term 'conspicuous consumption.' But keep your voice down. The loving couple are within shouting distance. And they definitely know how to shout."

He looked down the creek, where, at the moment, newlyweds Patrick and Candace were feeding stale bread to a gaggle of Canada geese that had landed at the far end of the Potter property. Patrick was a good-looking jock type, and Candace had that young Eva Marie Saint *On the Waterfront* look. Except richer. Much, much richer. Clearly Patrick's background was much more humble. And, clearly, the newlyweds were already at odds over it. Or something. In any case, they'd arrived at the B and B scowling at each other.

Now that peace—real or feigned—reigned, their videographer Alexis flitted around, filming them for posterity. Candace leaned into Patrick and he bundled her up in his sheepskin jacket, kissing the top of her perfect blond bob. Alexis caught the moment for posterity.

"I think I already saw this on The Romance Channel," Pacey mused.

"Hard to believe you'd tune in to that," Dawson said.

Pacey shrugged. "You know how Deputy Doug coos over a good love story." Dawson shook his head at that. For years Pacey had been making jokes that his older brother Doug was gay. As far as Dawson knew, that was a total falsehood.

An hour later, the Sumo brothers were installed in their rooms. Thus far, there had been no signs of broken box springs. When the newlyweds had arrived and Joey explained about the sleeping arrangements, Patrick had hemmed and hawed to Joey about having to sleep in a house on the other side of the creek. He'd wanted everything to be perfect for his new bride, he'd told them. But when Dawson pointed out what a spectacular view of the sunset they would have from their bedroom window, Patrick had mellowed out about it.

Now, Dawson and Pacey were trying to figure out how to ferry the three people and their copious belongings across the creek. It obviously couldn't be done in one trip.

"If I ever get married and decide to bring a videographer along on my honeymoon," Pacey told Dawson, "I am hereby giving you permission to declare me mentally unfit to handle my own affairs." He peered down the creek at the newlyweds. "How old do you think they are, anyway?"

Dawson shrugged. "I don't know. Young. Really young. Nineteen, twenty?"

"Twenty," said a voice behind them. Jen.

"Hey," Dawson greeted her. "What'd you do, ask them?"

"Yep. That chick Alexis is eighteen—information she volunteered, by the by." Jen glanced over at her. "She's cute, in a disgustingly preppie-trying-too-hard-to-be-artsy kind of way, don't you think?"

Dawson regarded the girl as she flitted around the newlyweds. The late afternoon sun glinted off her dark hair, which fell in a perfect line at her chin, and he noticed, yet again, how truly striking she was. She was very slender, with flawless porcelain skin. When they'd shaken hands earlier, he'd noticed her cornflower blue eyes, which matched her blue cashmere sweater.

"She's great looking," Dawson said.

Jen made a noise of disgust. "Dawson, Dawson, Dawson. Stick a strand of pearls around its neck and you mistake it for class."

"You just said—" Dawson began.

"Sarcasm, Dawson," Jen said. "Noun. In the dictionary. Look it up."

"A little testy, are we?" Pacey asked. "What stray hair has made its way up your bootie?"

"I seem to have taken an instant dislike to the girl," Jen admitted. "Perhaps it's her striking resemblance to Kathie Lee Gifford in a dark wig."

Pacey winced. "Kiss of death."

"Anyway, hurry up, you two," Jen went on, "because the college professor and her grandkiddies just showed, and they need to get ferried across, too. Joey and Andie are attempting to cook, so I'll stall them for a while. But get a move on, okay?"

"Aye-aye." Pacey saluted her. "And might I add that I don't see you as the play-with-the-grandkiddies type."

"Then you don't know me very well," Jen told him sweetly, as she turned on her heel. As she headed back to the house, she added over her shoulder, "Especially since these grandkiddies are male, eighteen, and incendiary."

Dawson scratched his chin as Jen strode up to the house. "You think she ever described either of us as 'incendiary'?"

"How many ways can you say 'no'?" Pacey replied. He pulled his jacket closer around his neck. "It's freezing out here, my friend. How about if you bring this stuff across, unload, and row back here. Then you can bring the four of them over to your house."

Dawson looked dubiously at the overflowing boat. "And lug all this crap up to my house by myself?"

"Think of it as free weights," Pacey suggested. "You know how the babes go for manly pecs."

"You're retrogressing, Pacey."

Pacey nodded. "Thank you."

An hour later, Dawson was puffing hard, making multiple trips from the dock on his side of the creek up to the house to haul the newlyweds' belongings and the videographer's gear up to his house. In spite of the cold wind that had blown up, he was sweating. It took so long that on his final trip, he could see Pacey at the oars of the skiff, rowing the Whites and their baggage over to Jen's house.

Dawson took a quick glance at the White guys. Okay, they were decent looking. So what?

"That's it," Dawson announced, as he brought the last two bags to the house. Patrick, Candace, and Alexis were sitting comfortably on the porch swing and chairs, sipping some lemonade that Dawson had brought them. "Let me take you guys inside and get you settled."

"I'll wait here, if you don't mind," Alexis said to him.

"Fine," Dawson told her. "This won't take very long. Patrick, Candace, if you'll just follow me." He opened the door for them and then followed them inside.

"Nice place," Patrick commented, taking in the cheery wallpaper. "Homey. Don't you think, Candace?"

"It's lovely," she agreed.

"Thanks." Dawson led them toward the stairs. It seemed weird that this couple he'd just met would be sleeping in his parents' bedroom.

"Isn't this nicer than camping, Patrick?" Candace asked, looking around, as Dawson led them upstairs.

"It's not exactly my dad's camp in the woods," Patrick agreed, but he didn't sound too happy about it. "You see, Dawson, I wanted our honeymoon to be a fishing trip to that cabin on the Moose River. But my bride nixed it."

"Patrick, that's private," Candace admonished. "I just wanted to have a honeymoon where I can take a shower or a bath."

"The cabin has a wood stove," Patrick protested. "It's easy to heat water. What are you so upset about? It's not personal information."

"It is to me," she replied.

Gee, happy couple, Dawson thought.

"I'm sure you two will have a wonderful time here in Capeside," he told them diplomatically. "Whale Weekend is always a lot of fun. And anything that I can do to make your stay here more pleasant, please don't hesitate to ask."

Joey would be proud of me for saying that, Dawson thought.

"Anyway," Dawson added, as they reached his parents' room, "here's where you'll be staying."

He opened the door, and his jaw dropped. The room had been transformed. There were two bouquets of fresh flowers—one on a nightstand, the other on the table closest to the bay windows. There was a fruit basket on the nightstand, too. And, in an ice bucket on the floor by the bed, a bottle of sparkling cider was chilling.

"This is so lovely!" Candace exclaimed. "Dawson, did you do this?"

Definitely not. It had to have been my mom, Dawson thought. *But she'd been too busy at the restaurant to even make it home. So, who could have done it?*

"We wanted to make your stay in Capeside memorable," was all Dawson could come up with as a response.

"I am sure that Patrick and I are going to have a wonderful stay with you." She smiled at him warmly. "Thank you so much."

Dawson smiled back. In that moment, he could see exactly why Patrick had fallen in love with her.

"Whoa, Dawson! You've got ESPN-2!" Patrick exclaimed. He'd found the remote control and was flipping through the channels on his parents' TV. "Awesome." Candace bit her lower lip and said nothing, but Dawson could see that her feelings were hurt.

If it was my honeymoon, Dawson thought, *the last thing I'd be thinking about would be sports on TV.*

Then Patrick clicked the TV off and hugged his bride. Maybe he wasn't so bad after all. He lifted her chin for a kiss. "Well, I'll just leave you two alone, then," Dawson told them. "My friend Pacey is running the skiff over to the Potters'. If you want to head over there, just go down to the dock and wave your arms, okay? Don't worry, no one has drowned yet."

The newlyweds were too busy to reply.

* * *

When Dawson found Alexis, she was on the porch, smoking a cigarette. "Nice of you to come back," she said, exhaling a perfect smoke ring.

"Sorry it took so long." He waved away the cigarette smoke. "You ready to see your room?"

"Seeing as it's probably below freezing out here, the answer is yes." She took a final deep hit on her cigarette and dropped it on the porch, snuffing it out with the sole of her boot.

"I'm sorry, but this is a nonsmoking house," Dawson told her.

She stared at him. "You're kidding."

"If I had been kidding, I would have been funny," Dawson replied tersely.

"Fine, whatever." She gave her buttery leather suitcase a pointed look, which clearly meant Dawson should pick it up. He did. "Follow me."

She did. Up the stairs to Dawson's room. Inside, Dawson opened the door to his bedroom and put her suitcase on the floor near the closet. She opened the closet immediately. "Whose clothes are in here?" she asked.

He'd moved all of his clothes to one side so that there would be room for her things, but he hadn't taken them out.

"Mine," he replied.

Her lip curled in a half smile. "Interesting. Do you come with the room?"

He laughed in spite of himself. "Fortunately for you, no."

She cocked her head to one side and regarded him. "And how do I know that's fortunate?"

She's flirting with me, Dawson realized. At least I think she is. Why isn't there a flirting manual for moments like these?

"You'll just have to take my word for it," Dawson said. "So, if there's anything you need—"

"A cigarette comes to mind."

"Sorry."

She folded her arms and looked around. "I take it this is your bedroom."

"Right on the first guess."

She tested the bed with the palm of her hand. "Nice bounce action. Have you tested it?"

Dawson reddened. Was she implying . . . or was that just his fevered hormonally induced imagination on overdrive, over a woman he now knew he didn't even like?

This called for a quick change of subject. "So, are you in college?" Dawson asked.

She sat on his bed and crossed her legs. "Bryn Mawr. I'm a legacy."

"Meaning your mother went there?"

She nodded. "And about a zillion generations before her, too. Everyone knows everyone else's family. Highly incestuous. I think that's how Candace's mother knows my mother."

Dawson folded his arms. "If you don't like it, why did you go to college there?"

She laughed. "If you knew my mother, you wouldn't ask that question. Look, are you sure I can't have one little cigarette without traipsing outside into the cold? Please? Pretty please?"

"I'm sorry. My parents made the rule a long time ago," Dawson said. "And it's their house."

She sighed. "I need to quit, anyway. But they keep me from eating."

"Eating isn't a bad thing," Dawson said. "Some of my favorite things come on a plate."

She threw her head back and laughed. "You are a hoot, Dawson Leery. I may have to turn my video camera on you."

"Not if I turn mine on you first."

Her eyebrows shot up. "Meaning?"

"You're not the only one around here who can handle a camera."

"Oh, a filmmaker?" She gave him a mocking look. "And here I had mistaken you for an ordinary high school student."

"They're not mutually exclusive qualities." Dawson headed for the door. "Let me know if you need anything. As long as it doesn't have anything to do with smoking."

Or the bounce in my bed, he added mentally, as he shut the door behind him. The body might be willing, but the mind can't stand the chick.

Chapter 4

"Hello. Welcome to Capeside's Weekend of the Whales kick-off dinner. Hello. Welcome to Capeside's Weekend of the Whales kick-off dinner . . ."

Andie and Jen stood just inside the door to the firehouse, doing their perky best to welcome people as they arrived. Across from them, Emily LaPaz and Kiki Greenblatt were doing the same thing. They were the four volunteer greeters whose job it was to make all the out-of-towners feel happy and welcome.

It was an uphill battle. A storm had blown in and it was raining buckets, which meant that the dinner was going to have to take place inside the cramped firehouse instead of on the street outside. Ms. Thatcher, a professional event planner out of Boston whom the Chamber of Commerce had hired to run

Weekend of the Whales, gazed out at the rain, a grim look on her face.

"You'd think the bad weather was a personal affront to her or something," Andie told Jen.

"It is going to get really crowded in here," Jen pointed out. "If we'd been able to keep the firehouse doors open and if people had been able to kind of mill in and out—"

"But we can't and they can't," Andie said, shrugging. "I suggest we simply make the best of it."

There were already more than a hundred people crowded into the firehouse, most of them in the buffet line. Gale, Mitch, and two dozen other volunteers dished up food, cleared off tables and replenished the buffet. They all wore blue and white T-shirts that read I HAD A WHALE OF A TIME IN CAPESIDE. Andie turned to greet a young couple entering the firehouse hand-in-hand. "Hello. Welcome to the Weekend of the Whales kick-off dinner."

"Hi," the good-looking guy said jovially. "We've got quite the Nor'easter going on out there, huh?"

"Bad luck on the weather," Jen agreed. "You're Patrick and Candace, right? I'm Jen Lindley. I met you—"

"Excuse me, I need that angle," an imperious voice from behind them said. Alexis maneuvered in front of Jen, her video camera to her eye, forcing Jen back with a hip-check.

"You really don't need to video us all the time," Candace told her, obviously embarrassed by Alexis's behavior.

Alexis kept filming. "Your parents hired me to get

a world-class video for you. And to do that, I need as much footage as possible."

"Well, so sorry I was in the way of your creative masterpiece," Jen said sarcastically. She smiled at Patrick and Candace. "The dinner is buffet style. So just go help yourselves."

The couple thanked her and headed into the dinner, Alexis right behind them. Kiki Greenblatt made a face. "Not exactly Miss Charming, is she?"

"She reminds me way too much of the majority of girls at my boarding school," Jen said, shuddering. "Somewhere along the way they got the impression that the world and everyone in it runs for their convenience."

Kiki studied Alexis thoughtfully. "She's really pretty, though. You know, in that impossible rich-girl way."

"Trust me, Kiki," Jen told her, "it's highly overrated, and mostly show."

"I'd like to move two of you greeters into the firehouse and leave two of you at the door," Ms. Thatcher told them, as she nervously fingered the pearls around her neck. "I hear people complaining that bad weather is predicted for the entire weekend. Evidently a few are already talking about leaving early. Which two of you are the most charming?"

Jen shrugged. "I'm notoriously charm-free."

Ms. Thatcher nodded. "Excellent cutting wit. A lot of these people are very sophisticated. They might go for it. So you and you." She cocked her head at Jen and Andie.

"Have fun," Emily called to them as they waded into the crowd.

"Be personable, perky, and nice to everyone," Ms. Thatcher instructed them before rushing off.

"Those instructions have a certain Miss America-esque feel to them that evoke my natural gag reflex," Jen remarked.

"Well, for the good of Capeside, I say we both go do our best impression of Miss Congeniality." Andie plastered a huge grin on her face and marched resolutely over to one of the long tables. "Hello. I'm Andie McPhee and I'm—"

"—Beautiful." A guy who looked to be about seventeen or eighteen finished her sentence. He was great looking, dark hair and eyes, very Ben Affleck's younger brother.

And he had just told her she was beautiful.

"I was going to say that I'm one of the official hostesses," Andie said, blushing slightly. "Not that I don't appreciate the compliment, because I do. Not that I necessarily agree with you. I mean, I'm not entirely odious-looking. But on the other hand—"

The guy held up his hand to shut her up and laughed. "Beautiful and funny. Winning combo. I'm Jonathan White." He nodded at the older woman sitting next to him. "This is my grandmother, Dr. Dorothy White."

"Hello." She nodded curtly at Andie. Andie judged her to be in her seventies. Her gray hair was short and chic, her pantsuit clearly by some well-known designer.

"Nice to meet you," Andie said.

Jonathan cocked his head across the table. "And over there is my ugly brother, Michael."

"You shouldn't say that about your . . ." Andie stopped. Because except for the fact that he was wearing sunglasses, the "ugly" brother to whom Jonathan referred looked exactly like Jonathan.

"At the risk of stating the obvious—twins," Andie said. "And you've pulled that before."

"Guilty," Jonathan admitted.

"Except I'm usually the one who gets to say he's ugly," Michael added with a grin. "Would you like to join us?"

"I really think I'm supposed to—"

Jonathan was already moving an empty chair from another table next to him. He patted it.

Well, Andie thought, what can I do, be rude to two guys who look like Ben Affleck? She sat.

"So, you live in Capeside?" Michael asked.

Andie nodded. "I grew up in Rhode Island, typical 'burbs kind of thing, but I really love it here. It's a terrific town. Have you been to Weekend of the Whales before?"

"I was too busy before," Dr. White said tersely as she sipped her coffee. "And it's a little plebeian for my tastes."

"My grandmother is an oceanographer," Michael explained proudly. "One of the world's foremost experts on whales. She teaches at Provincetown Oceanographic Institute."

"How fascinating," Andie said.

"*Taught*, past tense, would be the correct form of

that verb," Dr. White said briskly. "I've been put out to pasture, something like an antiquated cow. And I do not moo gently into that good night."

"Isn't that discriminatory?" Andie asked. "I mean, if you're an expert, why would they—"

"It's a long and bloody saga," Dr. White said. "And not one I wish to relate at this particular moment." She looked at her watch. "It's getting late. What time do we congregate on the beach for whale-watching in the morning?"

"Breakfast at Potter's begins at six A.M." Andie said. "They serve until eight."

"Come on, Dorothy, don't go," Michael pleaded. "It's not late and you know it."

Andie looked confused. "Did you just call your grandmother 'Dorothy'?"

Dr. White nodded. "At my request. I've always found the idea of being called 'granny' rather unsavory. I look around for some sweet old crone in a rocking chair, knitting afghans. And I couldn't very well have my own grandsons call me Dr. White."

"I see your point," Andie said.

"Dorothy is one of a kind," Jonathan put in. At that moment, Jen and her grandmother came over to their table.

"And how is the White party faring this evening?" Jen asked.

"Great," Jonathan said. "Now," he added, giving Andie a significant look.

"Well, isn't that lovely." Jen wagged her eyebrows at Andie.

"Delighted to hear you're all in high spirits," Grams said. "I'm pleased to have the three of you as my houseguests for the weekend. If there's anything I can do for you, let me know." She hurried off to greet others.

"My grandmother is digging this big-time," Jen confided. "Grams is a natural-born innkeeper."

"You call her 'Grams'?" Dr. White grimaced.

"Yeah." Jen shrugged. "Is that somehow strange?"

"It's a long story," Michael told her with a chuckle.

Jen leaned on the table and smiled at him flirtatiously. "Maybe you'd like to tell me this long story in the not-too-distant future."

Dr. White rose from her chair. "I shall leave the four of you to follow your hormonal sap wherever it may lead. Have fun." She nodded at them and headed for the door.

"Did she just say 'hormonal sap'?" Jen asked.

Jonathan nodded. "She's what you might call colorful."

"Girls. Andrea! Jennifer!" Ms. Thatcher called. She scurried over to them, clearly upset. "What is going on?"

"We're entertaining the troops, as directed," Jen joked. "And it's Andie and Jen."

"Andie. And Jen." Ms. Thatcher entwined her fingers. "What the two of you are doing at the moment is called dating and mating, not meeting and greeting. Please make the rounds like the gracious co-hostesses that I know you want to be."

"Right," Andie assured her. "We were just about to co-hostess our way to the next table."

"Wonderful," Ms. Thatcher said, already eyeing a screaming baby across the room. "I knew I could count on you. I'm off."

"Duty calls," Andie said, getting up.

"Tell me, Michael," Jen asked flirtatiously, "do you enjoy the primal dating and mating ritual?"

"I've been known to."

She gave him a wicked grin. "Funny how much we have in common."

Michael cocked his head. "So Andie, you free later?"

Andie's jaw hung open. *He had said "Andie," hadn't he?* Jen Lindley had just openly flirted with a boy who was choosing to openly flirt with her, Andie, instead. Amazing. It wasn't that Andie didn't consider herself reasonably attractive. It was that Jen was the kind of curvy, sexy, self-confident girl who could pretty much get any guy she wanted.

"I'll be around all night," Andie said brightly, "co-hostessing my little heart out."

"Great," Michael said. "I'll catch you later, then."

"Not if I catch her first," Jonathan told him.

In shock, Andie backed away from the table. "Well, I'll just leave you two to fight over me," she said. "Bye."

She whirled around and half-ran toward the buffet, filled with happiness. Jen was right next to her. Andie sidled behind the vat of coleslaw and automatically started to help Mrs. LaPaz, Emily's mother, dish it out.

"Did that just happen?" Andie asked Jen.

"It did," Jen acknowledged. "Score two for you."

"Okay, those two guys are in the extremely hot to totally incendiary range, are they not?"

"They are," Jen agreed.

Andie's eyes slid back to them. Jonathan waved to her. "And correct me if I'm wrong, but weren't both of them flirting with me just now?" She plopped a blob of coleslaw on a kid's plate.

"Right again."

"Not to rub it in," Andie continued, "but they were flirting with me instead of with you, correct?"

Jen smiled. "Your powers of observation are astonishing."

"Just answer one question for me: Why? Let's face it, Jen, you've got the guy thing down. You want 'em, you get 'em. But this time, it didn't work. So I have to ask, what is up with those guys? I mean, what are they, blind?"

Jen nodded. "Half-right. Michael's blind, Jonathan isn't."

Andie smacked herself in the forehead. "The sunglasses. Indoors. At night. I figured he was just affected. You know, a Hollywood wannabe kinda thing."

"Nope. Blind."

"Okay, I feel like a big butt-hole right now," Andie said, coloring. "Blind would account for him picking me over you."

"You definitely do not give yourself enough credit, Andie," Jen told her. "Besides, both of them were hitting on you. And only one of them is blind."

"I guess that's true."

"Hey, ladies, we having fun yet?" Pacey asked, as

he replaced the empty vat of baked beans with a full one.

"You know what they say," Jen singsonged. "Beans, beans, they're good for your heart, the more you eat, the more you—"

"And we all know what rhymes with 'heart,' " Pacey said. "Why Lindley, how earthy of you."

"Whale-watching dinners do that to me," Jen said. She looked around. "All in all, I'd say things are going well, wouldn't you?"

The firehouse was jam-packed, but people seemed to be having a good time. Over in the far corner, a local band was setting up their equipment. At Capeside's summer romance festival, the specially made T-shirts for sale had been a big hit. This time they were selling tourist versions of the same I HAD A WHALE OF A TIME IN CAPESIDE shirts that Kiki and Andie wore, and a long line of people were waiting to buy them.

"Considering the overbooking and the inclement weather, I would agree," Pacey said. "But if this storm doesn't clear up by tomorrow, all bets are off."

"Excuse me, but you're out of rolls," a woman told Pacey.

"I'll go get some, ma'am," Pacey assured her and headed back to the kitchen.

"He's right about the weather," Jen admitted. She could hear the rain pelting down on the roof.

"Well, we'll just have to cross that flooded bridge when we come to it," Andie decided. "In the meantime, let's go co-hostess."

* * *

Dawson threw used paper plates and plastic flatware into a huge plastic trash bag.

"Thanks for pitching in, Dawson," Mitch said, as he hurried by with a tray of desserts. "Did your mom bring the decaf out yet?"

"Yeah, it's over there." Dawson cocked his head toward the dessert table. "Anyone still eating?"

"I think there's a few people outside."

"I'll check on them later."

"Great, Dawson, and thanks. I really mean it."

Alexis strolled over to Dawson. She watched Mitch walk away. "Nice. Your dad looks like he works out."

"He does." Dawson reached for more used paper plates.

"Does his son?" Alexis asked.

"It's not high on my list of priorities."

Alexis looped her glossy hair behind her ear. "So you're just naturally buff, then?"

" 'Buff' is not exactly how I would describe myself."

"Well, take the word of an impartial observer, then," Alexis said. She lifted her video camera and began filming him. He couldn't help but notice that she'd changed into a button-down pink sweater with the top two buttons undone, revealing a flimsy, silky-looking little top of some kind. And above that, some pretty silky-looking flesh.

"I wish you wouldn't do that," Dawson told her. "When Candace's parents hired you to make a honeymoon video for Candace, I don't think they had me in mind."

"Well then, I won't include this footage in the video. I'll save it for personal consumption." She lowered the camera. "Just out of curiosity, is there anything that's actually edible back in that kitchen?"

"This wasn't enough for you?" Dawson asked.

"I said 'edible,' " Alexis pointed out.

"I see. That was your clever way of disparaging the cuisine. Maybe you'll enjoy tomorrow's seafood dinner more. My parents' restaurant is catering it and their food is great."

"And where's the lucky lady who hops into bed with your hunky dad every night?"

Dawson wiped his hands on a dishtowel. "Not to be rude, Alexis, but why are we having this conversation?"

She gave him a smoky look. "It's called small talk, Dawson. Which leads to big talk. Which leads . . . wherever it leads."

"Sorry, Alexis, I don't think it's going to lead anywhere."

Her eyebrows went up. "Is that so. Are you gay?"

"You think that's the only reason a guy would say no to you?"

"Pretty much."

"Interesting point of view." Dawson reached for more garbage.

She pointed the camera at him again. "I would really appreciate it if you'd stop that," he told her.

"I'm picturing you without that sweater and jeans on," she purred from behind the camera. "Boxers or briefs, Dawson?"

Dawson felt himself reddening. It was disconcerting enough to be the one with a camera pointed at him instead of being the one behind the camera. He could see how the camera empowered her to say whatever she wanted to say. He knew that feeling. And he didn't like being on the other side of it.

"I'd really like to not have this conversation," Dawson finally said. "And I would appreciate it if you'd stop filming me."

She kept filming. "Why, are you shy?"

"Are you deaf?"

She dropped the camera. "Nasty much?"

Dawson sighed. He knew he shouldn't insult the girl. After all, at the moment, he was an innkeeper by extension, and if he really ticked her off, it would reflect badly on Potter's B and B.

"Testing, one, two, three, testing." The lead singer of the band, a young woman with a braid down to her butt, called into the microphone. Dawson noticed that Candace and Patrick were standing right in front of the band, their arms around each other's waists.

"You might want to get the honeymooners now," Dawson suggested, jutting his chin toward them.

Alexis smiled coolly at Dawson. "No need to tell me how to do a video. I'm very good at what I do, Dawson. At everything I do." She added a significant look, then walked away.

Yuh. Dawson hauled the full sack of garbage to the kitchen.

"I saw you hanging with the preppie ice goddess

out there," Pacey said, as he broke open a new bag of Styrofoam cups. "Possibilities?"

"Zero."

"There's something extremely sexy about her ice maiden thing, don't you think?"

"No, Pacey, I don't."

"For one paltry moment of your adolescence, try thinking with parts in your nether regions, my man. Join me in the moral cesspool that is a teenage boy's imagination."

"I believe I indulged more than the imagination with Eve, if you recall," Dawson told him. "So I think at this point, I'll be passing."

Pacey clapped him on the back. "As long as you pass 'em in my direction, my friend." He headed out of the kitchen.

Out of the corner of his eye, Dawson noticed his mom leaning against the edge of the stainless steel counter. "Mom? You okay?"

"Sure, I'm fine." She smiled wanly at him.

He peered at her. "You don't look fine. You're really pale."

"My stomach is just a little upset. Think you could make this pot of coffee for me?"

"Sure." Dawson measured coffee into the giant coffee maker. From the firehouse, he could hear the band's lead singer introducing the band.

"I'm Macey Adams and we're Macey's Aces. Welcome to the Capeside Whale Watching weekend. We'd like to kick off your weekend with a fun singalong and we want everyone to join in. Don't be shy. You can think of us as live karaoke and get on up here and sing into the microphone if you want to. Let's start off with 'I Get By With a Little Help From My Friends.' "

"Thanks for your help, Dawson," Gale said, smiling gamely. "Can you take the coffee out after it brews?"

"Sure."

The singing carried into the kitchen. Dawson knew this was one of his mom's favorite songs, but she was just standing there, gripping the counter.

"Maybe you should sit down, Mom." Dawson got her a chair.

She sat. "This'll pass in a minute," she assured him. "Why don't you go on out there and enjoy the music?"

"Gale? Are you okay?" Mitch had just entered the kitchen. He hurried over to her.

"I'm fine, really. You guys can stop hovering over me."

"I wasn't hovering," Mitch told her. "It's just that you—"

"Dawson, go enjoy yourself," Gale interrupted. "This is silly."

"But—"

"Go," Gale insisted. "No melodrama is necessary, I promise."

The firehouse was rocking with the strains of the Beatles tune. The singing was louder than the rain on the roof of the firehouse. People really seemed to be having a good time.

He'd have to call and tell Joey. She'd stayed home to take care of her sister and to get everything together for tomorrow's breakfast. He knew she'd be relieved to hear how well everything was going. Maybe this weekend would be a success, after all.

Chapter 5

"Chew, chew, chew, chew!"

It was coming from inside the firehouse. Dawson stood under an awning outside trying to get some fresh air. It was still raining, but at least the out-of-doors wasn't as hot and humid as the still-packed firehouse.

"Chew, chew, chew, chew!"

No, the chanting wasn't coming from inside, it was coming from out back. Sticking close to the side of the building so that the incessant rain wouldn't pelt him, Dawson drifted behind the building. Thirty or forty people stood in a ring under a canvas canopy. As he got closer, he saw that the ring of people surrounded a cedar picnic table and two benches. Dawson pushed his way through the chanting crowd. Firmly planted on the two benches were the four Sumo brothers, two on each bench. They wore matching red, white, and blue warm-up outfits, with the words SUMO POETRY: IT'S A SLAM embroidered on the backs.

In the middle of the picnic table was a giant stack of chicken bones and corncobs, the debris of a monumental amount of food. It was a culinary Eiffel Tower, a masterpiece of gustatory engineering. The stack had to be at least three feet high. Dawson watched in amazement as Elvis took mere seconds to power his way through another corn on the cob. When it was done, he carefully aimed for the top of the food debris heap and launched the corncob. It landed atop the pile with a satisfying *thwack*.

"Chew, chew, chew, chew!" the crowd chanted.

"Unbelievable," Dawson muttered.

"Ah, Dawson!" Freddie grinned, spotting him. He clapped Dawson on the back. "Great dinner."

"Plus it's all-you-can-eat," Elvis added. "My kinda meal." He lifted a thirty-two ounce plastic stein filled with iced tea to his lips. "Where's that tasty little Joey this evening?"

"She's being tasty back at Potter's," Dawson replied.

Ike and Mike, who sat across from Elvis, began pounding the table. "Chug, chug, chug!" they chanted.

Elvis looked grandly at the crowd. "You want me to drain it?"

The crowd joined in the new chant. "Chug, chug, chug!"

He obliged them by draining the iced tea in a single, gargantuan draught.

The crowd cheered.

"Good thing he gave up beer," Fred told Dawson.

Elvis reached for another drumstick and thigh combination and bit into it as the crowd egged him on.

"I think I'm having a *Babette's Feast* flashback," Dawson said ruefully.

Freddie laughed. "Either that or *Tom Jones.*"

"You know those movies?" Dawson asked, amazed.

"I know we look like four big ol' gluttons, Dawson, but we're poets, men of letters, inspired by the word."

The culinary carnage continued. Mike and Ike had moved on to dessert, and were consuming huge bowls of rice pudding to the appreciation of the crowd. Elvis patted his stomach and turned to Dawson. "Do you happen to know if that tasty pretty little mama back at Potter's is planning to cook us up major victuals for breakfast? It's the most important meal of the day."

Dawson looked at him dubiously. "Do you always plan your next meal while you're still eating this one?"

"Eating is kinda a hobby of mine," Elvis said grandly. "If I don't eat a big breakfast, I get very—"

"Hey, Dawson!"

Dawson turned around. Pacey was at the back door of the firehouse, motioning frantically to him. Whatever was up was clearly not good.

"Excuse me." Dawson ran into the firehouse, noting that the rain had finally stopped. Bizarrely, the firehouse was nearly empty. Even the food stations had been abandoned. Pacey was nowhere to be seen.

"I could have sworn a hundred people were in here just a few minutes ago," Dawson muttered to himself.

"Out there," Macey, the lead singer, told him. She and her band were packing up their equipment. "Or in there." She pointed to the area where the firetrucks were, which was off-limits to the guests.

Very weird. Why would a hundred people decide to spontaneously continue their dinner out in the mud? Dawson wondered. It made no sense. He pushed out the front door of the firehouse. There were dozens of people standing around. He swiveled his head in every direction, trying to find Pacey. But he was lost in the crowd. People seemed upset, but Dawson had no idea why.

Before he could find anyone to ask, a movie moment ensued, as several ambulances screeched to a stop at the edge of the crowd. EMS techs and a few Capeside policemen jumped out; one of them was Pacey's brother, Doug.

Dawson made his way over to him. "What's going on?"

Doug looked at Dawson as if he was crazy. "You're here, we got called, and you're asking *me* what's going on?"

Pacey materialized at his side. "You missed the barfathon to beat all barfathons."

"Someone ate more than the Sumos out back?" Dawson asked, still totally confused.

"Not exactly," Pacey said.

"Not to worry, Dawson," Doug reported. "It's just food poisoning. Your parents are going to be fine in forty-eight hours, I promise."

"My par—?"

At that moment, Dawson saw two stretchers being carried out of the firehouse by four paramedics. Gale was on one, Mitch on the other. Mrs. LaPaz and Mr. Dumford, two other volunteers who had been serving food, were being lifted into another ambulance.

Dawson shook his head. "Mom? Dad? What happened?"

Gale looked deathly white, but when she saw Dawson, she gave him a weak wave to show him that she was okay. "Sub sandwiches from Charlie's Shoppe," she managed. "We ate before the dinner started. Bad mayo, we think."

"You ordered dinner before you served dinner?" Dawson asked incredulously.

"It seemed to make sense at the time," Mitch said weakly, reaching out to pat his son's hand.

Dawson whirled around. At least a dozen people were being loaded into the ambulances. This was an utter disaster. "Where are you taking them?" Dawson asked the nearest paramedic.

"County medical center. Now, please give us a little space to work."

Gale groaned. Dawson reached for her hand. "Hang in there, Mom." He turned to the paramedic again. "You sure my parents will be okay?"

"Son, they'll be fine," the paramedic assured him.

"Dawson, don't worry. When we get them loaded, I'll give you a lift to the medical center." Doug stepped in alongside Dawson as Dawson followed the stretchers carrying his parents. "How many people got sick?"

Pacey stood next to Dawson. "Yeah, I'll say people are having a real whale of a good time."

"How many got sick?" Dawson asked again.

"A dozen, I think," Pacey said. "Most of the main volunteers. Even that party-planner lady, what's-her-name—"

"Ms. Thatcher?" Dawson asked. "But she's in charge of everything!"

"Well, I'm sure they'll give her a nice, cozy hospital room right next door to the mayor's."

"The *mayor?*" Dawson asked.

"He was trying to pitch in and be a good sport," Pacey explained. "I guess ol' Charlie's not gonna get a whole lotta tourist business this weekend."

Dawson pressed close as his parents were loaded into the back of one of the ambulances. Mitch tried to get up off the stretcher and climb in under his own power, but the paramedics insisted that he allow them to load him in.

Dawson went to climb into the ambulance with them, but Gale stopped him. "Honey, we're going to be fine. Just call us at the hospital later." She groaned and held her stomach as another cramp hit her.

"But—"

"You've got a houseful of guests to take care of for the Potters," she gasped. "We'll be fine."

"Mom, you're ghost white and clutching your stomach—"

"We can't let Joey down," Gale managed.

Dawson watched helplessly as the ambulance took off. He felt a hand snake around his waist. It belonged to Alexis.

"Not very pretty, is it," she said, wrinkling her nose.

He moved smoothly out of her embrace. "That's not exactly my major concern at the moment." He noticed Jen standing nearby. "Did any of the tourists get sick?"

"Thankfully, no," she told him. "Grams is okay, too. She didn't eat the subs because she ate at home earlier, she said."

Patrick and Candace walked over to Dawson. "Are your parents okay?" Candace asked, obviously concerned.

"They will be," Dawson replied.

Candace rubbed her arms. "I think I'd like to just pack it in. Can we get a ride back, please? And maybe some tea back at the house?"

"Oh, sure." Dawson was momentarily nonplussed. He hadn't thought to get car keys from either of his parents, which meant driving their cars was, for the moment, not an option. He spotted Pacey, but the Sumo brothers were standing by, and they would definitely take up all the room in Pacey's truck.

"I'll take you back," Jen said, quickly catching on to Dawson's predicament. She turned to Patrick and Candace. "If we squeeze, I can fit the White twins and you guys. Or else I can come back for you."

"Squeezing is fine," Candace said graciously.

Alexis put her hands on her hips. "What am I supposed to do, get lashed to the roof?"

Jen looked thoughtful. "Now, there's an offer I can

hardly refuse. Did you bring your own lashing rope, by any chance?"

"I'll find you a ride, Alexis," Dawson said quickly. There was no point in antagonizing her any more than she was already antagonized, not with everything else that was going on.

Alexis eyed Dawson and smoothed some hair behind her ear. "And would you, by any chance, be riding in this car?"

"Sure. Excuse me. I'll be right back." Dawson took off, looking for Emily LaPaz. He knew Emily had her own car and had arrived separately from her mom. So, unless she'd gone to the hospital, maybe Emily could drive them back.

Suddenly, the full weight of the predicament hit him. He was now the sole proprietor of Potter's B and B extension, Dawson's Inn. And he had absolutely no idea what he was doing.

"How many eggs do you think the Sumos can put away?" Jen asked Joey, as she cracked another one into a huge pot and started scrambling it into the others. "We've got, like, four dozen eggs in here already."

"That's probably a snack for Elvis," Joey replied. "There's another dozen in the fridge. Pacey, how are you coming with those potatoes?"

Pacey held up his thumb, which had a fresh Band-Aid around it. "Oh, aside from the fact that I managed to hash my finger instead of the potato, I'd say I'm doing pretty well. Three dozen potatoes hashed and accounted for. Just out of the idle curiosity of the wounded, why didn't you try to borrow a food processor?"

"I am not Andie," Joey said. "Cooking is not one of my life skills, Pacey. In other words, it never registered on my frazzled little brain that such a thing existed and is used to shred such things as potatoes. Dawson, oranges?"

"Four dozen juiced," Dawson reported.

Joey fell into a chair. "Hopefully, this will cover the Sumos." She looked at the clock. It was after midnight. "Time for round two. Now we can start getting together breakfast for the rest of our guests."

"What happened to the pancake concept?" Jen asked.

"It's still a go," Joey said, "but the Sumos would have gone through all that pancake batter before the first cock crowed. And please spare me the verbal innuendos concerning my bird of choice."

"No cock jokes," Pacey said solemnly. "And the pancake batter has already been battered by yours truly. I did it before I hashed skin into the Tater Tots."

"Thank you." Joey let her head loll back against the wall and closed her eyes. "I am one whipped puppy. Not that I have time to indulge my whipped puppyhood." She sighed. "I should be thankful for small favors. Alexander has been a sweetheart."

"Maybe because he's getting his mom's undivided attention twenty-four hours a day," Jen pointed out.

"Maybe." Joey opened her eyes. "How long did the doctor say Gale and Mitch would have to stay in the hospital, Dawson?"

Regardless of his mother's instructions, Dawson had gone by the hospital earlier. His parents had both been asleep, rehydrating IVs in their arms.

"Dr. Brawnly said one night, maybe two. Has anyone checked the latest weather forecast?"

Wordlessly, Joey turned on a small radio on the counter. It was set to the news/talk station in Boston.

". . . It looks like steady rain will continue for the next twenty-four to thirty-six hours, as a low pressure system making its way up the coast appears to have stalled a hundred miles south of Block Island. We're expecting anywhere between two and three inches during this period; good news for the reservoirs, not such good news if you have plans to get out for the weekend. And that's your WBZ weather."

"Maybe there's an opposite to *The Rainmaker,*" Jen mused. "Some magnificent fellow who shows up in Capeside and magically makes it sunny."

"Might I remind you that *The Rainmaker,* or as he was more commonly known by the musical-loving filmic masses, *The Music Man,* was a charlatan," Dawson said.

Joey stood and stretched, then rubbed her lower back. "Debating the relative merits of movie musicals is not going to help out the predicament we're in. And somehow I don't think that the tourists who came for 'A Whale of a Good Time' are going to be happy with a Scrabble tournament."

"Excuse me." Mrs. Martino stood in the doorway, wrapped in a silk designer robe.

Joey jumped up. "Yes. Can I help you with anything?"

"Presumably. Your *guests* in the room next to ours are making some very strange noises. I can't possibly sleep under these conditions."

"Next door to you would be Elvis and Fred," Pacey said.

"I don't care if it's Bill and Hillary, I'd like some peace and quiet," Mrs. Martino said, her voice steely.

"No problem, Mrs. Martino," Joey assured her. "I'll take care of it."

Without so much as a "thank you," Mrs. Martino turned on her heel and left. Joey rolled her eyes to her friends and hurried after the irate woman.

When Jen was sure Mrs. Martino was out of earshot, she said, "So, do you think she acts like she acts due to terminal sexual frustration, or is the woman simply a bitch?"

"I'm voting bitch," Pacey said.

"Sex," Dawson decided.

Jen laughed. "Or both."

Down the hall, Mrs. Martino stood outside of Fred and Elvis's room, crooking her finger at Joey. "Just listen."

Joey waited. And waited.

"I don't hear—"

Suddenly, she did hear it. It sounded like a large woodland creature caught in a steel trap.

"There! You heard it!" Mrs. Martino cried triumphantly.

"Yes. I heard it." Joey took a deep breath and knocked hesitantly on her guests' door. "Hello?" she called.

The door opened. Elvis stood there in perhaps the

world's widest white terrycloth robe, sashed at what would have been his waist. He was guzzling from a sixty-four ounce plastic bottle of Coke. His eyes lit up when he saw Joey. "Pretty mama, The King is in!"

With his free hand, Elvis reached for Joey's wrist. She feinted away just as Elvis let out a belch that could be heard on the other side of the creek.

"That's disgusting!" Mrs. Martino sputtered.

"Natural bodily function, uptight mama," Elvis said. "Fred and I are working on a poem." He hoisted the bottle of Coke. "Gotta swig with the gig."

From behind him, where Fred was tapping away on a laptop, he waved to Joey. She waved back. "Um, I'm sorry, but no loud noises after midnight. House rules," she added. "Thank you very much for your consideration. Good night."

She closed the door and turned to Mrs. Martino. But the woman had already disappeared back into her room.

Dawson came walking down the hallway. "Everything okay, Joey?" he asked quietly.

"All things being relative, yes," Joey whispered. "The King's Coke was backing up on him, and Attila the Honey has gone back to bed."

He smiled at her. "You ought to get some sleep, Joey. We can—"

Elvis's door swung open. Elvis leered out at Joey and began a poem. "No one makes me hotter than a girl called Potter, she can scratch my itch, she ain't no bi—"

"And no improv slam poetry after midnight, either," Joey added firmly.

Elvis looked crushed. "That's my art."

"And I'm sure it's very artistic," Joey said sweetly.

Elvis eyed Dawson, then looked back at Joey. "What happened to the other guy, your boyfriend?"

"You mean Jack," Joey filled in. "He's . . . waiting for me. In the living room," she invented. "Which is why I have to go."

Elvis nodded and shrugged to Dawson. "Hey, you and me, man, the losers. That Jack is one lucky son of a gun." Still shaking his head, he closed the door.

Dawson eyed Joey. "And the story behind that is—?"

"Let's just say that a girl does what she has to do, Dawson."

"But a girl could have asked me to pose as her boyfriend, since the very obvious need arose."

"Jack was here. You weren't."

Dawson folded his arms. "That the only reason, Joey?"

She sighed. "It's irrelevant, Dawson. All I care about right now is getting through this weekend and making enough money to pay our mortgage, okay?"

"Okay." Dawson led the way back toward the kitchen, and then he turned to her and walked backward. "But it won't be irrelevant forever, Joey."

Chapter 6

Beep-beep-beep.

Joey groaned and put the pillow over her head, but it didn't drown out the relentless beeping of her alarm clock. Five o'clock in the morning was a truly hideous time to wake up.

She forced herself out of bed and padded over to the window. It was still pouring, the rain slashing out of the sky in huge sheets. After the food poisoning disaster of the night before, it would have been nice if nature had thrown them a bone and given them sunny skies for a day of whale-watching. But clearly, nature was in a foul mood and did not intend to cooperate.

Which means I'm about to serve breakfast to a dozen really ticked off whale-watchers, Joey thought. She took a quick shower with the water colder than usual so that she could save their hot water for the guests, then pulled on some jeans and a sweatshirt.

As she hurried downstairs, the smell of brewing coffee hit her. But that was impossible. They didn't own a coffee maker with an automatic timer on it. Which had to mean that Bessie had hobbled downstairs on one foot to—

"Morning!" Andie called cheerfully, as Joey came into the kitchen. "Want coffee?" She was arranging autumn leaves and flowers in a vase. Standing next to her was Jack, who was busily filling creamers. They both looked wide awake.

"What are you guys doing here?" Joey asked.

"Well," Andie began, "we figured since Dawson and Jen had Potter's B and B guests, and Pacey is running cross-creek transportation in the pouring rain, the least we could do is to come early and help you serve. Here. Drink. It's supercharged high-test." She handed Joey a cup of coffee.

"You didn't have to do this," Joey protested, but she took the coffee gratefully. "I mean, it's incredibly generous and thoughtful, but—"

"But what, you gonna kick us out?" Jack asked. "It's raining."

Joey smiled ruefully. "I had terrible dreams all night about hungry Sumo wrestlers turning on me while I tried to serve them burnt French toast. It got ugly—I think cannibalism was involved."

"People, people who eat people . . ." Andie sang, as if she were Barbra Streisand. She carried the coffee urn into the dining room and plugged it in, then hurried back to the kitchen.

"You're very perky, very early," Joey noted. "In fact, too perky." She helped Jack carry creamers into the dining room while Andie set the floral centerpiece.

Andie shrugged. "I'm just in a good mood."

"Plus she's a morning person," Jack added. "It's really hideous." He surveyed the table. "Okay, table's already set, coffee's brewing, creamers, sugar, artificial sweetener on the table."

From outside, there was a rumble of thunder. Joey winced. "Bad omen from the weather gods. They didn't say anything about thunderstorms, too."

"This bad weather is going to break," Andie said firmly. "I just know it."

"I hope you're right," Joey said. "If it doesn't, Mrs. Martino will probably hold me personally responsible."

"She is—?" Jack asked.

"In Room One with her husband. She eats nothing but kelp, something like that, and looks right through the hired help, also known as me."

"What's next?" Andie asked.

"I need to make fresh fruit salad." Joey led the way back into the kitchen and began taking fruit out of the refrigerator. "I figured if I made it last night it would look brown and gunky by now."

"If you squeeze a little lemon juice on cut-up fruit it won't turn brown," Andie said.

"Don't ask," Jack groaned. "My sister tapes Martha Stewart and plays it back while she's sleeping."

Andie began slicing the bananas. "Scoff all you like. Cooking good food with excellent presentation is all part of being the consummate hostess."

"Consummate away as far as I'm concerned," Joey told her. "Can you rinse off those grapes, Jack?"

"Good morning, beautiful innkeeper!" Joey didn't have to turn around to know who that was. Elvis.

Be nice, she told herself.

"Good morning, Elvis," she said, smiling at him over her shoulder. "We don't start serving breakfast until six, but you can help yourself to coffee or tea in the dining room."

" 'When love kicks in, gotta greet it with a grin, gotta go for gusto, it's a must-o, your life's a bust-o if you ain't in the mood for food, don't wanna be rude, but when I look at Joey, I get kinda crude.' " Elvis looked them over. "What, no applause?"

Andie and Jack looked at him like he was insane.

"Improv slam poetry," Elvis explained. "It's my specialty."

"And quite a special specialty it is," Joey said.

"Thanks." He bopped toward her as he invented another poem. " 'I look at you, I ain't no fool, 'cuz thoughts of sinnin', get my blood spinnin', for Joe with the mo, 'cuz she ain't no ho—"

"Elvis, Elvis, I am so glad you came down early," Joey exclaimed. She grabbed Jack and pulled him over to their mammoth guest. "I wanted to introduce you to my long-term, very serious boyfriend. Elvis, this is Jack. Jack, this is Elvis."

Elvis sighed, then put out his hand. "Hey man, you are one lucky dude. She is hot."

"Don't I know it," Jack said with deadpan earnestness. "Wow."

Elvis held his palms up. "I'm not about stompin'

on your turf, man, tasty as it might be. Catch you later." He turned and went into the dining room.

Andie looked at Joey. "What was that?"

"One of the Sumo brothers," Joey replied. "There are four. And he's the smallest." She turned to Jack. "Thanks for becoming my boyfriend, by the way."

Jack offered a half-smile. "Kinda like old times."

"Kinda," Joey agreed.

It seemed so strange now, to think that she and Jack had been a couple right after she'd broken up with Dawson. Which was before Jack finally admitted to himself—and to everyone else—that he was gay.

"So, tasty turf," Jack teased, "How about if I put the fruit salad out."

"I'll get you for that," she called after him.

"What next?" Andie asked.

"Let's see . . . pancake batter is already made. We should put out the little cereal boxes and the granola. Get ready to cook the scrambled eggs and hash browns from last night." Joey checked her watch. "Pacey is picking up Patrick, Candace, and Alexis in ten minutes, so we should hustle."

"So, when is Pacey ferrying Dr. White and her grandsons over?" Andie asked casually.

"The next trip, I guess. Why?"

"No reason." Andie carried the cereal boxes into the dining room, then built a pyramid with them. "They're very nice."

"Who?" Joey asked, as she set cups of fruit-flavored yogurt into a serving bowl filled with crushed ice.

"Michael and Jonathan White. Did you know Michael is blind?"

"No!" a male voice said dramatically from behind them. "Why didn't anyone tell me?"

Joey and Andie turned to see Michael in the doorway. Andie clapped her hand to her mouth. "Okay, I am monumentally embarrassed right now."

Michael laughed. "Are you blushing?"

"I can confirm that she is," Jack said, as he swung his way back to them from the kitchen.

"Andie, there's nothing to be embarrassed about," Michael assured her. "I was teasing you. See, I really already knew that I'm blind."

"I know you knew," Andie said. "But I didn't know you knew I knew. Something like that."

"I thought you were part of ferry load number two," Joey said.

"Change of plans. The newlyweds were otherwise engaged, and I wanted to get over here so that Andie could tell me I'm blind." He grinned in Andie's direction. "And that's the whole story. Good morning, Andie."

"Good morning, Michael." She grinned back at him, even though of course he couldn't see her. She found herself thinking that he looked even cuter today than he'd looked yesterday. "Can I get you some coffee?"

"How about if I get *you* some coffee?" Michael suggested. "Just tell me where it is."

Andie eyed the breakfront where the coffee urn was set up. "Well it's . . . how can I tell you when you won't know what I'm talking about?"

"Pretend I'm the center of a clock. Straight ahead of me would be high noon, straight behind me would be six o'clock. So, what time is the coffee and about how many paces?"

"Uh . . . three o'clock, and about ten paces."

"Cool." Michael made his way confidently over to the breakfront, felt for the coffee urn, and filled two cups, judging how much coffee was in the cups by the heat rising from the hot liquid. He held one out to her. "Or do you take cream and sugar?"

"Black is fine. That was very impressive."

"Good." He took a sip of his coffee. "Because I was trying to impress you."

Mrs. Martino strode into the dining room. "It's raining," she announced flatly. Joey looked over at her. She was dressed all in black, which matched the scowl on her face.

"It is," Joey confirmed. "But hopefully it'll clear up. Can I get you a cup of coffee?"

"Herbal tea." She pulled out a chair and sat, arms folded, waiting to be served.

Joey colored. "Um . . . I'm sorry, Mrs. Martino, but I don't have herbal tea, just regular Earl Grey."

"For goodness sake, how can you call yourself a bed and breakfast and not offer herbal tea?"

"Audacious of me, I know," Joey said before she could stop herself. "Excuse me." She hurried to the kitchen and took a deep breath. This was no time to lose it. There was simply too much to do. She pulled the pancake batter out of the refrigerator and poured oil into a pan as Pacey came into the kitchen.

"First mate Witter reporting for duty. The newlyweds are, euphemistically speaking, sleeping in, Dr. White says she never eats breakfast, and Alexis is in the front hall trying to convince Dawson to join her in a low-budget remake of *Love Story*. I knew there was something vaguely Ali McGraw-ish about her."

Joey stirred the pancake batter. "Thankfully, Dawson is no Ryan O'Neal, with or without Ryan's recently acquired beer gut. And someone might want to point out to Alexis that not only did Ali die in that movie, she also played a poor girl." She thought for a moment. "On second thought, don't mention it."

Pacey regarded her thoughtfully. "That wouldn't be a slightly green-tinged remark, would it, Potter?"

"As in, am I jealous? Don't be ridiculous." She reached into the refrigerator for the scrambled eggs.

"So you just dislike her on general principle, then? Would you say that you'd dislike her an equal amount if she was hitting on, say, me, instead of Dawson?"

"I haven't given her any thought one way or the other, Pacey. I'm just a little overwhelmed here at the moment, in case you failed to notice."

"Chill, Potter." He picked up a spatula. "I'll flip pancakes. You go make nice to the guests. Except for you-know-who."

"Sometimes you are extremely annoying." But Joey took his advice and went into the dining room. The Martinos were sitting at one end of the long table, as Mr. Martino sipped some coffee and his wife scowled out at the dark day. Along the far side of the table, the Sumo poets were eating massive bowls of fruit salad topped with mounds of yogurt.

As for the fruit salad that Joey had laboriously made, that bowl was already empty.

"Hey, great fruit salad!" Fred told her. "It lasted fifteen seconds."

"Thanks." Joey found herself idly wondering where Dawson and Alexis might be. They were nowhere in sight.

"Miss, do you at least have some fresh juice?" Mrs. Martino called to Joey.

"Yes, ma'am, the carafes of grapefruit juice are right next to the coffee."

"It's made from *concentrate,*" Mrs. Martino snapped.

"That's true," Joey replied.

Andie was sitting next to Michael at the other end of the table. "If you section a grapefruit and squeeze just a little fresh in, it really does mask the concentrate taste." Mrs. Martino looked at her as if she'd just passed gas. "Or not," she added lamely. Michael cracked up.

"Do the whales even come out when it's raining?" Mrs. Martino asked.

"Seeing as they live in the water, I don't think rain will deter them," Joey said. "Okay, the pancakes, eggs and hash browns will be out shortly." She turned to head back into the kitchen just as Dawson and Alexis came in, laughing together about something. Alexis shook her head, and her wet hair flung droplets of water on him.

"How great do my pancakes look, Potter?" Pacey asked Joey as she slammed into the kitchen. He eyed her, then flipped a pancake. "Hey, we're havin' a whale of a good time now, huh? On the *Pequod* they ate hardtack and salt blubber and all kinds of other things, by the by."

"Everything is fine. Just fine. And if you want to eat what they ate on the *Pequod,* that's fine with me, too." She reached for another skillet and poured eggs into it. "Scrambled eggs for four hundred and seven coming right up. The Sumos count for one hundred each."

Jack carried some empty bowls into the kitchen. "Elvis just asked me how long we've been a couple," he reported. "He also wanted to know, *mano-a-mano,* just how far we'd carried the lust-filled side of our relationship. I told him I don't kiss and tell."

"Change of orientation when I wasn't looking, Jack?" Pacey asked.

Joey shot him a killer look. "I asked Jack to pretend to be my boyfriend so that 'Love Me Tender' in there won't decide to turn his quarters upstairs into Graceland's Jungle Room with me."

Pacey deftly slid pancakes onto a platter and poured more batter. "You could have asked me, Potter," he said casually. "I wouldn't have found the charade entirely odious." Jack discreetly walked out of the room.

"Jack was here, Pacey," Joey told him. "You weren't."

"I see."

"As is abundantly clear by your tone of voice, Pacey, you don't see," Joey snapped.

"I guess there's just Something About Joey," Pacey quipped. "And your eggs are burning."

He was right. She shoved a spatula underneath the

yellow mass and turned it over. Too late. It was brown, almost black. She poured it into the sink and started over. Dawson walked into the kitchen. "Morning. What can I do to help?"

"Can you make eggs?" Joey asked.

"Sure."

"Great. Make 'em." She handed him the spatula and grabbed the first platter of pancakes, then looked at him over her shoulder. "Unless you're too busy with the cashmere-clad videographer to pitch in, that is."

"Joey, I don't even like the girl," Dawson protested.

"Well, great, that makes two of us." Joey stomped into the dining room with the pancakes.

Pacey poured more pancake batter. "She is not a happy camper."

Dawson melted some butter in the pan. "Aside from near-death food poisoning of half the good citizens of Capeside, and the typhoon that has currently taken up residence outside, I thought things were going really well."

"Here's the update, Dawson. Pretty much nothing is going well. Oh, one other thing. Joey and Jack are back together."

Dawson eyed Pacey. "I assume that's only part of a statement."

"Assume away."

"And the rest of it would be—?"

"Ask Joey," Pacey suggested.

Dawson turned the eggs. "I'm a little tied up at the moment."

"So I see. And why would you need an explanation at this exact second, my friend?"

Dawson made a face. "I don't believe I said I did."

"I don't believe you said you didn't."

"Pacey, this is a ridiculous conversation."

"You're right. Ain't teen angst fun?"

Chapter 7

Clad in a yellow rain slicker, Dawson stood on the dock in the pouring rain. He wiped the water from his face, but it was pointless, since he was instantly dripping wet again. The rain was falling as if it had a personal vendetta against Capeside. Or whale-watching. Or both.

"Whale-watching on the *Capeside Queen,"* Burke Reese, the first mate of the *Capeside Queen,* called from the deck of the boat. It was almost impossible to hear him over the rain. "Whale-watching on the *Capeside Queen! Capeside Queen* departs in five minutes! Whale-watching on the *Capeside Queen!"*

Good luck, Dawson thought. He could probably throw in a Darryl Hannah-esque mermaid, circa *Splash,* and still not get very many takers. The *Capeside Queen* was an eighty-five-foot party fishing boat that doubled as a whale-watching vessel between April and early November. The rain, which actually had let up for a bit between eight and nine-thirty, had intensified again, and the sky was slate gray. There was no sign of impending sunshine.

"Keep it up, Burke," Dawson shouted to him. "You're doing great."

A couple in matching clear plastic rain capes stood on the deck, huddled under an umbrella. A camera dangled from the man's neck as if it would ward off evil spirits.

"You folks planning to get on the boat?" Dawson asked.

"You gotta be crazy to go out on a boat in this weather," the man said.

"Maybe it'll be fun, honey," his wife demurred.

"I'm against whale-watching in the rain, and that's that. Big waste of time driving all the way up here from North Carolina, is how I see it."

"You really should go out," Dawson urged. "You'll have a great time. And the weather around here can change in nothing flat."

"Not for me, buddy," the man insisted. "Come on, Wella, we're heading back to the camper." They hustled off.

"Two more lost to the land, when they could have been lost to the sea," Andie said, walking over to Dawson. "Well, I say quitters don't deserve to see Moby Dick."

"And since when are you such a woman of the sea?" Dawson asked.

Andie smiled. "Since Professor White and her

grandsons said they're going out on the boat, no matter what."

Dawson nodded. "And it wouldn't be Professor White who induced this decision?"

"If you are implying that I have motives other than the fact that Joey asked us to accompany the B and B guests on the boat, the answer is: none of your business," Andie replied. "So what about you, you up for it?"

"Frankly, the last thing I'm up for is to board this vessel, motor twenty miles out into the middle of Cape Cod Bay in search of oversized mammals who probably have the good sense to stay as far below the surface as possible for the maximum time between breaths."

"You're not going?"

"In a moment of utter insanity I seem to have agreed to Joey's request," Dawson said. "Which means a boat ride is in order."

A gust of wind pushed rain into both their faces. "Did you take a Dramamine?" Andie asked. "You know, for motion sickness. With this wind, it could be rough out there."

Dawson shook his head regretfully. He hadn't thought about motion sickness until Andie had just mentioned it. But she was right. The winds were gusty. Gusty winds meant choppy seas. Choppy seas meant a good chance of a choppy stomach.

Like it isn't bad enough that both of my parents are still in the hospital recovering from their mayo-induced barfarama, Dawson thought. Just the thought of the waves now made his stomach queasy.

"Yo, Burke!" Dawson called up to the first mate. "How long we going out for?"

"Four hours," Burke responded, sounding none too happy about it.

"That's what the brochure said," Andie confirmed. "We leave at ten sharp, we're back at two o'clock, we go to the Stellwagen Banks feeding grounds, and the *Capeside Queen* has a ninety-nine percent success rate of seeing whales."

"Whale-watching on the *Capeside Queen,* whale-watching on the *Capeside Queen. Capeside Queen* departs in three minutes! Whale-watching on the *Capeside Queen!*" Burke was pleading now. "Best whale-watching on the eastern seaboard. *Capeside Queen!*"

Poor guy, Dawson thought. He understood why Burke was feeling a little desperate. Whale Weekend was a big source of revenue to the tourist industry during a time of the year when most tourist dollars dried up. But if the *Capeside Queen* couldn't book a decent number of fares for the trip, they'd spend more money on diesel fuel to and from the whale grounds than they'd take in. It was no way to make money.

"Hey!" a bearded tourist called to the first mate. "Is there any other place to see the whales? We had reservations with you for today, but you gotta be nuts to go out in this weather, bro."

The mate shook his head. "If the weather's good, you got a shot out at Dunn's Lighthouse, on the bluffs. The Oceanographic Institute puts a big telescope at the top of the lighthouse. But now, with this fog, forget it."

"Miles, you told me the whales come right up by the beach," whined a woman whose head was obscured by a huge umbrella. "You told me you can see them from the shoreline."

"I'm telling you, honey, I came here when I was a kid and saw whales right from the beach," her husband insisted.

"You got extremely lucky, then," Dawson told them. "The last two years, you could see them from the lighthouse, but that was unusual. Your best bet for a prime whale-watching experience is to get on the *Capeside* . . ."

He stopped mid-sentence, because the couple was already walking away.

"Don't take it personally, Dawson," Andie told him, patting his arm through his rain slicker. "I am just so impressed with Professor White, aren't you? Did you hear her explaining to the other guests that there'd be far less boat traffic on the bay on a bad day, which meant the whales would be less skittish?"

"Heard the coverage," Dawson assured her dryly.

"Yo, landlubber!" Elvis the Sumo poet called down to them from the deck of the boat. "When we getting this party afloat?" Fred, Mike and Ike joined him, waving wildly.

"Two minutes," Dawson called back up to them. "We're just waiting to see if anyone else shows."

"Let's see," Andie began, ticking people off on her fingers. "The newlyweds decided to stay in bed, there's a shocker for you. The ever-gracious Mrs. Martino is definitely not venturing out in this, and her hubby is staying behind with her. Pacey, Jen, and

Jack are helping Joey clean the place and get ready for dinner, so I'd say we're ready to shove off."

Professor White appeared off the stern of the boat. "Mr. Leery, are you what's holding us up?"

"We'll be aboard in just a second," Dawson assured her.

"Capeside Queen, departing in one minute!" Burke bellowed, his voice now echoing around the nearly deserted marina. During the past few minutes, there had been a large exodus of tourists.

"Okay, okay, let's go," Dawson told Andie tersely. "It is only four hours. Maybe we can work it into our *Moby Dick* papers somehow."

"You know, Dawson," Andie told him, "there was a huge storm in *Moby Dick,* too. Captain Ahab had St. Elmo's fire form all around him in it as the deck of the *Pequod* pitched to and fro. In fact, there was almost a mutiny and the boat almost capsized and—oops, sorry."

From behind, someone covered Dawson's eyes with their hands. He got a sinking feeling in his stomach. He turned around. Alexis, clad in a Ralph Lauren raincoat, grinned at him. "Were you going to leave me in your bedroom all alone?" she asked him.

"I was under the impression that your job is to be wherever Patrick and Candace are. And they aren't here," Dawson said.

"True. But since they're spending the day in bed, and they didn't invite me to join them, I'm free to join you." She pulled up one side of her raincoat to reveal her video camera. "Have camera, will travel."

"Let's rock 'n' roll, Dawson," Burke said.

Dawson, Andie and Alexis stepped off the gangway and onto the *Capeside Queen*. With a loud blast on his foghorn, the captain gunned the engines of the *Capeside Queen* as his mates cast off the bow and stern lines.

The boat putt-putted out of its slip and into Capeside Harbor. The whale-watching voyage was underway, whether Dawson liked it or not.

Andie and Michael stood in the galley, trying to keep their balance. "You sure you don't want to go back up on deck?" Andie asked, as she handed him a steaming mug of hot chocolate.

"Nah. Seen one roiling sea, seen 'em all," Michael joked.

Andie sipped her cocoa. From where she stood, she could see into the cabin. Most of the ship's passengers were in there, talking, sleeping, trying not to get sick. Professor White and Jonathan were up on deck with a handful of other intrepid, waterlogged souls.

"Well, that girl is certainly a piece of work," Andie commented, peering into the cabin. "I'm referring to Alexis."

"The one with the affected voice?" Michael asked.

"Now that you mention it, she does sound affected, doesn't she. Well, she's in the cabin with Dawson. He's sitting there with his eyes closed, clearly trying to ward off seasicknesses, and she's actually videoing him."

"You think he doesn't know?"

Andie shrugged. "I think he doesn't like, that's for sure."

Michael leaned against the counter. "There's a certain kind of rich girl from a certain kind of privileged background—they usually have a certain kind of totally predictable good looks—who find it impossible to believe that any guy could possibly resist them. I have a feeling that applies to Alexis."

Andie eyed him. "Just tell me to shut up if this is a really crass question, but how would you know that she's good-looking?"

"Mental telepathy?"

Andie laughed. "I'm serious."

"Okay then, seriously. I could see until two years ago."

"Oh my God, that's horrible!"

Andie thought for a moment. "Wait, how could I say that? Why would I find it horrible that you could see for the first fifteen years of your life? Jump in here and tell me to shut up at any point, Michael."

"Don't be so hard on yourself. It's a very common gut reaction," Michael assured her. "I think it's because now you know that I know what I'm missing. And before you ask the next obvious question, the answer is: car accident. My best friend was driving. He got thrown from the car. I got stuck. They couldn't get me out before it blew up."

Andie reached for his hand. "That really *is* horrible."

"Feel badly for me, huh?"

"Of course I do!"

"Really, really badly?"

"Really, really."

He leered at her comically. "I'm not above a pity make-out session."

She laughed and playfully punched him in the arm. "You are truly demented."

"So I've heard." He reached one hand out and touched her face. Slowly, he traced it with his fingertips.

"Oh God, this is just like *Butterflies Are Free!*" Andie exclaimed.

"Like what?"

"This old movie with Goldie Hawn. She falls for this gorgeous blind guy and he feels her face to see what she looks like. I always loved that part."

Michael smiled. "Me, too." He touched her face again.

"She told him she looked like young Elizabeth Taylor." Michael's fingers traveled down her cheek, gently touching her lips. "As luck would have it, I look just like Angelina Jolie."

"What does she look like?"

"Oh, that's right. She got famous after you went blind. What I meant to say is, I look just like Winona Ryder."

"My educated fingers tell me that you don't look like anyone but you, Andie."

"Yeah, I guess." Andie thought for a moment. "Most everyone you meet is shallow. Meaning that people get attracted to people based on their looks. But you can't see what I look like, so . . ."

"Maybe I'm not so shallow," Michael said.

"But then why would you like me when you don't know me?" Andie blurted out. "Not that I'm objecting to your liking me. I mean, I like that you like me, but—"

"My brother told me how pretty you are," Michael confessed.

"He did?"

"Yes," Michael said. "And no. Yes, he did. But only after I told him that I liked you. Then he said he liked you. Then we fought a manly duel for your affections. Finally, I had to throw him overboard."

"So now he's swimming with the fishes, eh?" Andie asked.

"Not with the whales, evidently. It doesn't look like any are going to show up."

Andie took another sip of her hot chocolate. "Strangely enough, I don't find that a major disappointment."

Michael smiled and reached for her hand. "Strangely enough, neither do I."

Dawson groaned. He'd started to feel queasy not more than fifteen minutes from the docks. And the ill feeling had intensified as soon as the *Capeside Queen* reached open water. The seas were running four to six feet, and the vessel had started pitching violently from side to side. Dawson found himself a quiet corner near the galley and tried to ride it out. He'd pretty much sat there for the entire trip so far. Fortunately, he hadn't eaten that much for breakfast.

He tried to decide if opening his eyes would make him feel better or worse. He decided to risk it. Alexis had a video camera in his face.

"What are you doing?" he asked her.

"Guess."

"I would appreciate it if you would refrain from videoing me now, Alexis."

"I've already got lots of footage. I never knew there were quite so many variations on the color green that a person's skin could turn. This could be an award-winner."

"I'll alert the people at Cannes." The boat hit a rough patch of water and Alexis lost her balance, colliding into Dawson's arm.

"Sorry," she said, but she didn't move away. So he did. She laughed. "You are just so amusing."

"Good to know I've got high entertainment value. So you know how much longer we'll be out here?"

"An hour. Then we'll head back."

"An hour," Dawson responded. "That's a lot of seconds."

"You might feel better if you looked at land," Alexis suggested. "While you were sleeping earlier, that's what Professor White suggested we all do. Something about the inner ear being balanced."

"Looking out at the land would entail getting up and going out on deck, neither of which appeals at this particular moment. Plus, there's the fog."

"Not anymore," Alexis said. "It's cleared off. A little, anyway. Professor White is up there doing the naturalist play-by-play. The regular oceanographer is too seasick to talk." She set her camera down. "Seriously. Come on outside, you might feel better."

He eyed her dubiously. "You sounded almost human for a moment there."

"You don't think a great deal of me, do you?"

Dawson remembered his resolve not to alienate

her. But it was probably already too late. "I don't really know you, Alexis," he hedged.

"True. And let me make something abundantly clear to you. I'm not in the habit of panting after small-town high school boys with small-minded ideas and even smaller life experience."

"Well, if that little diatribe is supposed to apply to me, then I would have to say: you don't really know me, Alexis."

"Exactly." Her eyes met his. "Isn't it insulting and annoying when someone who knows nothing about you presumes they know everything about you?"

Meaning that's what I'm doing to her, Dawson thought. *And she's right.*

"Point taken. And I apologize."

She leaned over and kissed his cheek. "Apology accepted." She reached for his hand. "Come on. Let's go up."

Dawson managed to stand. "I'm coming. Any whales?"

"Not a one. Professor White says there's still a good chance." She led him outside into the cold salt air. It had actually stopped raining, though it looked as if it could start again any minute. Alexis inhaled deeply. "See, not so bad, huh?"

"Dawson!" Freddie hailed, as soon as he saw him. "Come fish with the Sumo brothers!"

"Get Dawson a line," Ike instructed Mike. "Dawson, we're catching dinner for everyone tonight while we wait for the whales to show."

The Sumo brothers were not kidding. They stood along the starboard rail of the *Capeside Queen,* sturdy boat rods under their arms. Dawson watched as Freddie let drop a two-ounce diamond jig nearly to the bottom, and then pumped it up and down with his massive arms. Suddenly, the rod bent nearly in two.

"One on!" Ike called. "One on!"

Freddie started reeling like mad, as people gathered from all over the boat to watch. His rod shook violently as the fish fought to get away. "Sand shark," Burke said knowledgeably. "They fight like that."

But the first mate was wrong. As the fish neared the surface, he told them it was an Atlantic cod, and a pretty big one at that—at least ten pounds, maybe fifteen. The mate went for a gaff, and then neatly brought the cod on board.

"Dinner!" Ike said proudly. "Dawson, does Joey know how to gut and clean a fish?"

Before Dawson could answer—fortunately, since he was completely certain that Joey had no intention of gutting a fish—Professor White's voice boomed out over the *Capeside Queen*'s public address system.

"Whales! Whales! Two o'clock, three hundred yards, two o'clock! Ladies and gentlemen, we have two humpback whales at two o'clock!"

All the people on board rushed to the port side of the boat, where the well-constructed vessel handled their weight easily. They scanned the sea as the boat bobbed up and down on the swells, looking for—

"Dawson! Look! There they are!" Andie was pointing to the distance.

"Where?" Dawson asked. He didn't see anything but the slate gray sea. And then he saw them—two mottled shapes and a distinctive flash of white, as one of the humpbacks flapped its tail.

"They're coming this way," Professor White told everyone, obviously relishing her impromptu job as shipboard oceanographer and naturalist. "Two hundred yards, now. They see us. They're closing, they're coming to say hello! Thank all the other boats for staying in the harbor, because these whales are fearless!"

"Amazing. Truly amazing." Dawson's seasickness was instantly forgotten. He stood transfixed as the whales approached. They were enormous, with long flippers below their heads.

"There's one with his head out of the water," Andie explained to Michael. "Oh, I wish you could see it!" Jonathan was on the other side of Michael, describing everything for his brother.

"The whale with his head out of the water is spy-hopping," Professor White explained. "Watch him spin as he does it; it gives him a chance to have a look around." As she described what he might do, the whale started to spin around, as if on cue.

"Awesome," Andie breathed.

KER-SPLASH! One of the whales jumped high out of the water not more than forty yards from the *Capeside Queen,* and then crashed back to the water's surface with an enormous impact.

"A breach," Professor White said calmly. "He might be playing, he might be showing off to his buds, he might be loosening skin parasites."

"Elvis'll dive in and ask him!" Ike joked.

"He really might," Andie muttered. "Elvis is bigger."

The group watched, transfixed with the wonder of the giant mammals. Alexis got so involved that Dawson had to remind her to film it. For a half-hour or more, three and sometimes four humpbacks cavorted near the *Capeside Queen*. Then, each of them breached in turn. And then, they were gone, disappearing as quickly as they had appeared.

Their timing was perfect, because the wind and rain picked up again, rocking the *Capeside Queen* so strongly that the passengers had to grasp the handrails for safety.

"The captain requests that all passengers return to the cabin," Professor White told them calmly. "All passengers, to the cabin. We're heading for home."

Dawson went to help Michael, but Andie and Jonathan were already there, guiding him toward the open door to the main cabin. As Dawson stepped inside the cabin door, the engines of the *Capeside Queen* growled loudly, and the captain expertly turned the vessel back toward the harbor. For the next hour, they motored through choppy waters. Fifteen minutes outside the harbor, the rain started anew.

Right before they docked, Andie said to Dawson, "Funny, huh? This trip turned out to be a success after all. Wasn't that the most amazing thing to see, Dawson?"

"It was. Joey will be so sorry she missed this."

"Pacey, too."

Dawson smiled ruefully, thinking how natural it seemed that Joey and Pacey should be there, no matter how all their respective relationships had changed. He sighed.

"That's the way it goes, Dawson," Andie said, staring off the bow. "That's just the way it goes."

Chapter 8

KA-BOOM!

The old-fashioned Revolutionary War-era cannon at the east end of the Capeside town green fired a ceremonial blank round, as Ms. Thatcher's replacement, Lydia Gerkin, president of the Capeside Pride Society, looked on approvingly from the small stage that had been erected nearby.

"Let the games begin!" Lydia proclaimed. The meager crowd of two hundred or so people who had gathered on the green applauded half-heartedly. Despite being dressed in all variations of rain gear, they were mostly soaked. It wasn't pouring; instead, they were dealing with a steady, relentless drip.

Dawson sighed. In other years, when the weather had cooperated, the annual Whale of Fun events on the town green on the Saturday afternoon of Whale

Weekend was a major event. In addition to the hundreds who came for the entire weekend, a good thousand or more people from the surrounding area would show up for the day of games, open-air food booths, and musical performances. This year, though, the horrendous weather had put a real damper on the turnout.

Nonetheless, Ms. Gerkin was determined to carry on. Whale of Fun was going to commence, rain or shine.

It was an hour after the *Capeside Queen* had docked at the marina. Jen had been at the dock to meet the vessel. She delivered a plea from Joey for Andie to come back to the B and B at four to help her get dinner ready. Andie, Joey had said, was the only one of her friends she felt certain actually knew how to cook edible food. As for Jen, she was supposed to stay at the Whale of Fun events with Dawson and help entertain the disgruntled masses.

Andie looked at her watch. "That still gives me a couple of hours before she needs me."

"Good," Michael said, grinning. "You up for some more hot chocolate?"

"Sounds great." The two of them headed off toward the concession stand.

"I'd like to stop home and change clothes," Dawson told Jen. I'm thoroughly drenched."

She handed him a small dishtowel. "I'm like a Girl Scout. 'Be Prepared' is my motto. Blot dry."

Dawson took the towel and dried his hair. Up on the makeshift stage, Ms. Gerkin was giving a lively speech about all the fun things that would take place that afternoon. It wasn't exactly going over well.

"Poor Lydia," Jen said. "Her big moment in the sun, rained out. I don't suppose you saw any whales out there?"

"We did, actually. You want this towel back?"

Jen took it. "Moby actually showed?"

"Multiple Moby, Jen. They were magnificent. I'm sorry you missed it."

"Me, too."

"We'll go again," Dawson assured her. "Sometime when the weather is better." He looked around. "They probably should have canceled all of this, or postponed it, or something. I mean, this is pitiful."

"No, pitiful would be getting food poisoning from some bad mayo and spending two days barfing your guts out in the hospital. Speaking of which, Dawson, how are Gale and Mitch?"

"Much better. I called them early this morning. The doctor is going to release them tomorrow morning. So, how are the guests who stayed behind?"

"At the B and B? They're hanging in there," Jen told him. "But I think if the Martinos hadn't paid for the whole weekend in advance, they'd have left by now, too. Joey's expecting Mrs. Martino to start screaming 'refund' at any minute. Fortunately—or unfortunately—Mrs. Martino hasn't been seen since breakfast."

"Maybe Mr. Martino got inspired by *Eating Raoul,*" said Dawson.

"You win, Dawson. You have just referenced a movie I do not know," Jen admitted.

"It's a hilarious black comedy about a couple who kill people and then grind them up for food."

Jen held her stomach. "Suddenly I feel like I swigged some of that bad mayo."

"I know we're not going to let a little weather get in the way of Whale of Fun, are we?" Ms. Gerkin exclaimed into the microphone. They were some half-hearted yells of support.

"Terrific! Let's think positive until Mother Nature changes her game plan. Why, this is just a little . . . liquid sunshine!"

"Liquid sunshine?" Jen echoed dubiously.

Dawson shrugged. "We'll have to at least give her points for spirit in the face of the underwhelming."

"We shall begin the Whale of Fun with a special presentation," Ms. Gerkin said, clasping her hands together. "I've been watching these delightful, talented people rehearse for this moment for weeks now, and I admit I'm just a little biased, but this is just so super. Please welcome the Capeside Community Players in a special dramatic reading of Herman Melville's *Moby Dick: or The Whale.*" She applauded enthusiastically. A handful of people joined in.

Jack, Andie, Jonathan, and Michael appeared at their side, sipping their hot chocolate. "Is this really happening or are we all having the same nightmare?" Jack asked, as local actors dressed in nineteenth-century whaling garb made their way out onto the stage.

"I didn't enjoy reading the novel; I certainly don't want to be put through the anguish of hearing amateur actors reading it," Jen said.

"I say we reserve judgment," Andie said firmly.

One of the Community Players, who had a long,

obviously artificial beard, stepped forward from the line of actors, and assumed a dramatic pose. Then, with a loose-leaf notebook cradled in one arm, he began to declaim in stentorian tones:

> Chapter One: Loomings. Call me Ishmael. Some years ago—never mind how long precisely—having little or no money in my purse, and nothing particular to interest me on shore, I thought I would sail about a little and see the watery part of the world.

"To see a watery part of the world, you wouldn't have to leave Capeside!" someone shouted from the back of the crowd.

Jen snorted back a laugh. "Hecklers?"

"That's horrible!" Andie said.

Jen shrugged. "But funny."

The audience evidently thought so, too, as many of them were tittering. The actor playing Ishmael looked flustered. However, he plunged ahead.

> It is a way I have of driving off the spleen and regulating the circulation.

"Don't tell me about circulation, buddy!" the heckler yelled. "You shoulda seen what was circulating at the firehouse Friday night. I think someone barfed up their spleen!"

This time, the crowd roared with laughter. "I'm sorry, that guy's a riot," Jonathan said between peals of laughter.

"But it's so mean," Andie protested.

Dawson craned his neck but he couldn't see who the heckler was. "While I might share his sentiments, I find it repugnant to heckle an actor, even a really bad actor. I mean, look at the poor guy."

Up on stage, the actor playing Ishmael was flushed with humiliation. He had to wait for the laughing crowd to quiet down. He took a deep breath and then started once more, reading from his notebook.

> Whenever I find myself growing grim about the mouth;
> Whenever it is a damp and drizzly November—

"Yeah, like today, buddy!" the heckler bellowed. This time, the crowd absolutely convulsed with laughter.

"Look, even Ms. Gerkin is laughing!" Jen pointed to the plump, little woman who stood to the side of the stage, having herself a merry old time.

"Poor Ishy," Michael said, laughing.

Dawson couldn't help it, he felt badly for the guy. He decided to find the heckler and shut him up. In the nicest possible way, of course.

"Be back." Dawson pushed his way through the crowd, trying to find the heckler. Meanwhile, the show, such as it was, went on.

> . . . whenever I find myself involuntarily pausing before coffin warehouses, and bringing up the rear of every funeral I meet; and especially

whenever my hypos get such an upper hand of me—"

"I'd like to give a hypo to the heinie who ordered up this weather!"

The crowd lost it, falling all over itself in mirth, trying to see who the hilarious heckler was. Dawson saw a ring of people surrounding someone—the heckler, he figured. He pushed his way through. "Hey, buddy," Dawson began, parting the crowd, "don't you have any sensitivity to . . ."

His voice trailed off. Sumo Brother Fred sat there, holding a loose-leaf notebook that matched the ones the actors on stage had. "Hey, Dawson!" Fred greeted him. "Is this a riot, or what? You wanna play my part for a while? It's a hoot!"

Dawson stopped short. "You mean, this is all part—"

"Of the show," Freddie filled in, whispering. "Someone recommended me to Ms. Gerkin up there and they gave me the script when I got off the boat." He glanced down at the page. "Oh wait, I've got a line coming up."

If they but knew it, almost all men in their degree, some time or another, cherish very nearly the same feelings toward the ocean with me.

"Yo, I got those ocean feelings again. Bring on the Dramamine, baby!" Freddie yelled.

This time the laughter from the crowd stopped the show. The actor on stage slunk off, completely mortified.

Ms. Gerkin hurried to the microphone. "Ladies and gentlemen, a round of applause for our wonderful heckler, Fred!"

Everyone turned in Fred's direction, recognizing now that they had been suckered by the Community Players. Fred jumped up and down and waved to the crowd as they cheered for him.

All Dawson could do was laugh. It had been the highlight of the Weekend of the Whales thus far.

". . . On to our next fabulous event," Ms. Gerkin announced into the microphone after a half-hour break, during which a whole bunch of kids asked Fred for his autograph. "The next fun event is the whaling spear throw. The winner will receive a complimentary CAPESIDE IS ROMANCE T-shirt."

"Cheap much?" Jack asked.

"Plus dinner for two at the Capeside Manor," she added.

"Better," Jack acknowledged.

"All contestants please proceed to the south end of the town green for the whaling spear throw. Join in the fun, everyone!"

The whaling spear throw was an annual Whale Weekend event. Up until a few years ago, contestants had actually thrown spears at a giant sixty-foot wooden cutout of a white whale, aiming for the whale's heart. But after a group of high school students protested that whales were now an endangered species, the weekend organizers had changed the target. Now, the target was a twenty-foot high, ten-foot wide cutout of a snarling Captain Ahab look-alike.

Much more P.C., Dawson thought, as he headed for the other side of the green.

"You up for this, bro?" Michael asked Jonathan. " 'Cuz if you are, I was thinking that I might just have to kick your butt."

Jonathan leaned close to Andie. "I can take him with one hand tied behind my back," he told her confidently.

"I heard that," Michael said. "You're going down, bro."

Andie looked from one brother to the other. "You guys are kidding. Right?"

"Wrong," the brothers said together, but they were laughing as they said it.

Andie looked at Michael. "Michael, I appreciate your attitude. It's really exemplary. But how can you do this?"

He held his arm out to Andie. "Take it." She did. "Now, lead me to the whaling grounds, where I shall vanquish both your fears and my brother Jonathan."

"No chance," Jonathan insisted.

They made their way to the south end of the green, where the spear-throwing event was already underway. Elvis stood behind a white line about twenty-five yards from the cutout of Captain Ahab, spear in hand. Then, with a mighty yell, he ran up to the line and let the javelin fly.

THWACK! It smacked into Captain Ahab's thigh. The crowd cheered, but Elvis shook his head disgustedly. "I'm too strong for my own good," he said, as one of the organizers marked the place his spear had impacted with his name.

Jonathan took a spear and got in line. "Good luck, brother," Michael called to him. "You're going to need it."

Andie looked at Michael doubtfully. "Look," she said. "I appreciate your enthusiasm. But how—"

He cut her off with a wave of his hand, as his brother took two running steps toward the firing line and launched the spear at Captain Ahab. *Wham!* It stuck right in Ahab's left shoulder, not far from the heart. The crowd watching the competition applauded. It had been the most successful shot yet.

Michael leaned close to Jonathan. Andie could barely hear them—something about how many paces away Ahab was, and the angles involved. When Ms. Gerkin realized a blind contestant was about to throw the spear, she nearly fainted. The event organizers quickly tried to dissuade Michael, citing safety concerns.

"And so," Ms. Gerkin concluded, "perhaps this isn't the perfect event for you, Mr. White, considering your . . . uh . . . condition."

"What condition?" Michael asked.

Jonathan turned his head so Ms. Gerkin wouldn't see his snort of laughter.

"Well, your . . . your disability," Ms. Gerkin sputtered.

"Ma'am, I appreciate your concern," Michael said. "But I can see just as well as Captain Ahab. Plus, as you pointed out yourself, there are no humans anywhere near the target. I won't have to sue you for discriminating against the sight-impaired, will I?"

"No, goodness, no!" Ms. Gerkin cried.

Michael grinned. "Great." He stood at the throwing line. Word that a blind teenager was going to take a chance at spear-throwing had people flocking over. "Can somebody please go bang something against Ahab's heart? A hammer, a plate, a Frisbee, anything. Just loud enough so I can hear it."

"I'll do it," Andie called. "Just don't shoot until I give you the all clear." She hustled over to the cutout, pulled off her shoe, and banged the sole on Ahab's heart a few times. "Loud enough?"

"Once more," Michael instructed. He furrowed his brow in concentration as Andie hit the cutout a few more times. "Fine! Let me know when you're out of the way."

Andie sprinted to the sidelines, far away from the Ahab cutout, then she yelled, "Okay, I'm gone!"

Michael nodded in concentration. The crowd hushed.

Jen leaned close to Dawson. "You mean he's going to aim for Ahab's heart based on the sound he just heard? Is that possible?"

"I guess we're about to find out," Dawson replied.

Just as Michael was about to throw the spear, there was a loud cheer from the other end of the green.

"What's happening?" Michael asked.

"The Sumo poets are mud-sliding," Jonathan reported, peering down the green. "Freddie just ran for about fifty yards and launched himself on his belly into a huge pool of mud. I think he just knocked over an old lady from Palm Springs and her toy poodle."

"I hate it when that happens," Michael teased. He

took a deep breath, steadying himself. Then he took three solid steps toward Captain Ahab and let fly with the spear. His spear pierced the same spot on Ahab that his brother had hit. The crowd cheered wildly.

"How'd I do?" Michael asked, "where'd I hit him?"

Andie ran to him and hugged him. "You hit the same place Jonathan did. That is so amazing!"

"Not really," Michael said. "I wanted to beat him.

"But Michael, that's not exactly realistic."

Michael shrugged. "From my point of view, 'realistic' is highly over-rated. How many more contestants are there?"

"None," Dawson told him. "But Emily LaPaz's spear throw beat both of you by about two inches."

"Where is the wench?" Michael sputtered, pretending to be angry. "I'll go double or nothing."

"Too late, bro," Jonathan told him. "They're awarding her the winning T-shirt even as we speak."

"Bummer. Well, at least you didn't beat me," Michael told him.

"Next time, man." Jonathan pointed at Michael. "Watch your back."

Andie watched the brothers sparring with each other. It was so obvious how deeply they loved each other. *It's like how I feel about Jack*, she realized. *If anything ever happened to him . . .*

She shuddered. It was too awful to even think about.

Suddenly, she felt an arm around her shoulders. "Hey, sis."

Jack wasn't demonstrative very often. But now

Andie noticed that he was gazing over at Michael and Jonathan.

Andie smiled at him. "Hey."

"I was just thinking," Jack began, "that as siblings go, you are more than adequate."

That gave Andie her answer. Jack was thinking the same kinds of thoughts she had been thinking. She leaned against his shoulder. "Funny. I was just thinking the same thing about you."

Chapter 9

Joey sank into the nearest chair and surveyed the mounds of dirty dishes that covered nearly every surface of the kitchen. Her friends lolled around the room. She, Jen, Andie, Dawson, and Pacey had just finished serving dinner to their guests. They had mountains of dishes to show for it. Pacey had just left to row Dr. White, Patrick, and Candace back across the creek.

Michael, Jonathan, and Alexis were hanging out down by the creek, waiting for them to finish cleaning up. Jonathan had suggested they could all hang out together that evening, and Andie had thought of showing them all Dunn's Lighthouse.

"The innkeeper concept might be highly overrated," Dawson mused, eyeing the mess that surrounded them.

"Your parents own a restaurant, Dawson," Jen pointed out. "Dirty dishes are not new to you."

"True. However, the wonderful thing about staying in school is that you know that your professional dishwashing days are numbered."

Joey stood up and stretched. "Well, we might as well get it over with." She picked up a couple of dirty dishes.

"I'll rinse, you load, Joey," Andie said. "Dawson, take out the garbage. And Jen, you can wipe down the counters. And vacuum in the dining room. And mop."

"Was there some kind of mental checklist involved in this plan?" Jen asked.

"Oh, you know me, Little Miss Organized," Andie chirped. She went to the sink and began to rinse dishes, handing them over to Joey. "All in all, I'd say the dinner was quite successful, Joey. The lasagna turned out great—"

"I burnt the second batch, Andie," Joey said. "Lasagna isn't served blackened."

"Okay, well, the salad was super."

"Mrs. Martino found a bug in her lettuce."

"Funny how no one saw this alleged insect except her," Dawson said, as he tied a garbage bag closed. "I think Mr. Martino is married to a head case."

"The Sumos must hold world eating records or something," Jen guessed. "The amount of food those boys can put away is scary. At least they knew how to clean and cook their own fish."

Andie handed Joey another plate. "Look on the bright side. There are no messy leftovers to contend with."

"This perky thing of yours is going just a little overboard, Andie."

Andie shrugged. "Sue me, I'm happy. We'll need to soak the lasagna pan for a while."

"Captain Pacey, reporting for duty," Pacey said, as he strode into the kitchen. "Patrick and Candace are, and I quote, 'turning in early,' and Dr. White is going out with Grams."

Jen laughed. "You're kidding. The only place Grams ever goes at night is Bible study class. And it doesn't meet on Saturday night."

"Well, tonight they're going someplace non-church related. It seems your grandmother and the good professor of whales and other underwater mammals have bonded like the sisters they aren't," Pacey reported.

Jen scrubbed at a spot on the counter. "Don't tell me. They're gonna drag race down Main Street and see if any cute boys show up."

"They didn't confide specifics to me, Jen," Pacey said. "But I can tell you this much. Lipstick and perfume were involved."

Jen stopped scrubbing. "Lipstick? Perfume? *Grams?* These three nouns have not shared the same sentence before."

"I plan to wear lipstick and perfume when I'm her age," Andie said. "And I'll even wear skimpy red underwear."

"For some lucky old codger clad in bikini briefs," Pacey quipped. But he couldn't help picturing Andie in said red underwear, though in his mind she was as young as she was now. He had been so in love with her once. *Maybe Andie was right. Maybe you never truly got over your first love,* he mused.

He looked at Joey. *Or maybe the one you thought was your true love wasn't really your true love at all.* Everything between him and Joey was so—

"So, does that work for you, Pacey?" Dawson asked.

"What? Sorry, my mind was tripping the light fantastic," Pacey said.

"I said that I would be forever grateful if you could feign some interest in Alexis so she'll leave me alone," Dawson repeated.

Pacey nodded. "A beautiful, rich, intelligent, talented young woman, who is also, might I mention, deeply into film, is basically throwing herself at you, and you want me to pick up the slack?"

"Something like that," Dawson agreed. "Have you got any more garbage bags, Joey?"

"In that cupboard. Second shelf. Pacey, you failed to mention her shallow, self-centered, grandiose sense of entitlement," Joey pointed out. "Not that I don't find her charming or anything."

"Grandiose? Really?" asked a voice from the doorway.

Oh no, Joey thought. Because it sounded like—

"Hi, Alexis," Jen said quickly. "We thought you were down at the dock with the twins."

"Just my luck to traipse back here to use the john in time to hear Joey's bitter little diatribe against me."

Joey turned to her, blushing. "I apologize, Alexis. Probably the stress of the weekend just got the better of me."

"You think?" Alexis studied Joey coolly. "You have some lasagna on your T-shirt. There's a little in your hair, too. Just thought you'd like to know." It was all Dawson could do not to strangle the girl as Joey brushed at her T-shirt self-consciously.

"You're fine, Joey," Jen assured her. She turned to Alexis. "Why don't you just let us finish up here? We'll be down soon to get you guys."

Alexis pouted. "There's only so much time I can spend videoing a creek in the dark. Sadly, Patrick and Candace don't seem inclined to ask me to make salacious home movies of their honeymoon bliss. In other words, I'm bored. Can't Dawson come out and play?"

"Dawson is helping his friends clean up at the moment," Dawson said, through clenched teeth. "Dawson suggests that you go play nice with Jonathan and Michael."

Alexis leaned against the door frame. "For some bizarre reason, they both seem to be crazed for little Andie over there."

"None of us find that bizarre in the least," Dawson told her. "On the other hand, some of us find it bizarre that you seem to have this need to insult people you know absolutely nothing about."

"Not people," Pacey pointed out. "Girls. You only seem to rag on females in the nubile stage of development. At the risk of antagonizing the clientele, Alexis, you seem to have hostility issues."

Alexis laughed. "You're hilarious! Who knew a mind was lurking behind that Neanderthalish brow. I was only joking. Where can I buy a pack of cigarettes around here?"

"You can't," Joey said flatly. She turned back to the dishes.

"Seriously," Alexis said. "I'm not going to burn down your little B and B. Scouts' honor." No one answered her. Joey kept her back to Alexis. "Uh, excuse me, Miz Innkeeper? Don't they even have 7-Elevens or something like that on this side of the tracks? I mean, poor people smoke, don't they?"

The kitchen went deathly silent.

Jen put down her sponge and slowly walked over to Alexis. "I know you," she said softly.

Alexis's eyes widened. "From where?"

"I know all about you," Jen went on. "Your parents have handed you everything on a silver platter since the day you were born. You've had the right friends and you wear the right clothes and you go to the right school. And you think anyone who doesn't fall into your narrow little life view is somehow less than you. I've known you my entire life."

Alexis smirked. "Been looking in the mirror lately, Jennie?"

"As a matter of fact, yes." Jen stared daggers at her. "But the difference between you and me is, I now appreciate how truly poverty-stricken your life and your sort of person actually is. In short, Alexis, I am evolving. Whereas you are destined to spend your entire life as the shallow bitch you are right now. Have a fun day."

Red-faced with fury, Alexis turned on her heel and left.

"Now, that was great," Andie declared, as the rest of them stood in mute shock. "The mouth is mightier than the sword. I know it's supposed to be 'pen,' but the spirit is there."

Joey sighed, poured dishwashing powder into the dishwasher, closed it and turned it on. She couldn't look at Jen. " 'Great' is not the first word that springs to mind. She's a guest. It's our—I mean, my—job to be nice to her. No matter what we think of her. She isn't paying to be insul—"

"Come on, Joey—" Jen began.

"I didn't need you to defend me, Jen," Joey insisted. "So I hope you didn't feel the need to do that on my account."

"I didn't. I felt the need to do it on mine."

"Here's an idea," Pacey said. "Let's just blow the chick off. Sorry, Dawson, but I definitely cannot feign interest of any kind in Alexis, comely as her physicality might be. Life is too short to waste a nanosecond on her."

"I second that emotion," Dawson agreed.

"But she probably went back down to the dock with Michael and Jonathan," Andie reminded them. "And we said we'd take them out to Dunn's Lighthouse. They're probably waiting for us right now."

"Waiting for you," Jen corrected her. "The twinly studmuffins are slobbering in your direction, Andie."

Andie colored. "Well, I can't entertain the 'twinly studmuffins' all by myself, can I? And, unfortunately, Alexis isn't going to disappear. So can't we just make a valiant effort to have fun and ignore her?"

"Sure, Andie." Pacey draped an arm around her shoulders. "Why wouldn't we all want to help you out there?"

"We're just friends, Pacey," Andie assured him. "I mean, I just met Michael and Jonathan. And they're leaving tomorrow. And—"

"No need to explain, McPhee." Pacey kissed her cheek. "What do you say, wrong-side-of-the-creekers? Shall we go make merry with the paying guests?"

"Not that an evening under the cloudy skies of Capeside with Alexis isn't my idea of a swell time," Joey began, "but I should stay here in case any of the guests need anything. The Sumos could get an urge for a midnight snack. Mrs. Martino could see Elvis on the shower curtain, that sort of thing."

From upstairs, a baby began to scream. "Or a nephew could start screaming his little guts out," Joey added with a sigh.

"I can go up and check on him," Jen offered.

"No, you guys go have fun," Joey told them. "You've already helped me more than I had any right to hope for. It's stopped raining, at least temporarily. It'll be a nice walk. And by the end of tomorrow, which from my point of view cannot come soon enough, this will all be over."

An hour later, the group stood on the bluffs by Dunn's Lighthouse, which shimmered eerily in the fog.

"Amazing," Jonathan said. He quickly described it for Michael. Almost a hundred feet high, searchlights were trained on it from all directions. To get there, they'd crossed a boggy swamp by flashlight, though the town had laid down a crude wooden path that at least kept their feet from getting soaked.

"How old is it?" Michael asked.

"It dates back to the 1800s," Dawson said, "to the earliest days of whaling in this community. We almost lost it last year when some multi-billion dollar conglomerate was going to buy it and tear it down to build some kind of strip mall and resort thing, but the Nature Conservancy bought it and it's now safe forever."

"Wait, I read about this," Alexis said. "This is the lighthouse where that girl sat twenty-four hours a day to protest its being destroyed, isn't it?"

"Quinn Bickfee," Pacey filled in. "She sold the movie rights to her story to Lifetime."

"She's playing herself in the movie," Dawson added. "They already shot the picture, but they didn't use Capeside because it was too expensive. I think they shot it somewhere in North Carolina."

"To add irony to the mix, Quinn Bickfee got selected for *Survivor,*" Jen put in. "Who says fame is fleeting?"

"I read in *People* that *The Quinn Bickfee Story* is going to be during May sweeps," Andie said.

"And then to video." Jen tapped her chin with her forefinger. "Shall we watch on TV or shall we rent?"

"We shall protest the fact that they didn't shoot it in Capeside and boycott," Andie decided.

"In the larger scheme of things, McPhee, that's not very important," Pacey said. "Look at it this way. The Mighty Quinn's little publicity coup saved our lighthouse."

Dawson grinned. "Why, Pacey, if I didn't know better I'd say you were finally developing a certain fondness for your place of birth."

"It comes over me every once in a while," Pacey admitted. "Don't let it get around."

"So, can we go inside?" Alexis asked.

"It's not officially open now," Dawson said, "but come on in."

"Come on in, where?" Jen asked, even as they all followed him. He gingerly made his way toward the structure, leading them to the back of the lighthouse, where he pushed open a small, hidden door.

"Breaking and entering, Dawson?" Jen asked.

"The one and only Garth Beecher presides over the safety of our fair lighthouse by night. Remember him, Pacey?"

"You mean the G-man? The old guy who used to volunteer to help kids learn to read in grade school?"

"One and the same."

"But Dawson, if memory serves correctly, the guy was ancient way back when we were kids. By now he's got to be—"

"—Beyond ancient," Dawson filled in. "And he's the same nice, salty old guy he always was. He's the night watchman, comes by three times a night. He told me at the marina I could bring some people by, so we're covered on the breaking and entering thing. Come on."

They climbed up the dark, damp, circular stone steps, their flashlight beams piercing the darkness. "This place would be hell on asthmatics," Andie pointed out. "You okay, Michael?"

"I'm blind, not wheezing," he quipped. "Besides, I can see in the dark."

"Love that blind humor, bro," Jonathan said, clapping him on the back.

"Andie, I'm feeling dizzy," Michael said suddenly, reaching his hand out.

She grasped it quickly. "That's okay. I've got you." She huddled in close to him. He grinned hugely.

"I can't believe you fell for that, Andie," Jonathan groaned. "My devious brother just wanted to get next to you."

Andie frowned at Michael. "Is that true?"

"Hey, I'm blind, cut me some slack."

Everyone laughed and teased him as they finished climbing the steps. Dawson noted that Andie's hand was still in Michael's.

"When the fog thins out the view from up here is amazing," Jen said, as she led them into the watchtower. "On a night like this, though, you'll have to use your imagination."

They all stood there for a while, inhaling the salty night air. The lighthouse was inoperable, so they simple imagined the beams of light from the tower playing over the fog and water.

"If I was one of the Sumo brothers," Andie said, "this scene would inspire me to poetry. About old whaling ships, and widows walking on the bluffs, looking out to sea for ships that don't come in."

"It already is poetry," Dawson said quietly. "No words are necessary."

"You're right," Jen said, gazing out at the night. "Some things are just beyond words."

* * *

So tired she could barely remain upright, Joey picked up Bessie's dinner dishes and stood next to the bed. "You sure you don't need anything else?" Joey whispered so she wouldn't wake Alexander.

"I'm fine, Joe." Bessie looked at her blissfully sleeping son. "He looks like an angel right now, doesn't he?"

"Looks can be deceiving."

"I know." Bessie gently smoothed some hair from his forehead. "I want you to know that I'm really proud of you, Joey, for how well you're handling all of this. It's unbelievable, really."

"You weren't there for dinner. Believe me, Bessie, I've made tons of mistakes already—"

"Don't be so hard on yourself." She reached for Joey's hand. "Mom would be so proud of you."

Whether from exhaustion or sentiment, a lump filled Joey's throat. "She would have been so much better at this than we are, Bessie. Than *I* am, anyway."

Bessie smiled sadly. "Joey Potter, you happen to rock in a major way. And as soon as I can walk on this stupid ankle again, I am going to plan some kind of wonderful surprise to show you how much I appreciate everything you're doing."

"If the weather doesn't clear up tomorrow, we could have big problems," Joey warned her. "The only people who saw whales were the ones out on the *Capeside Queen*, and half of them got seasick. In other words, I doubt that we'll have repeat visitors next year."

Bessie shrugged. "Joey, if there's one thing I've

learned in the last few years, it's not to sweat the stuff you can't control. Whatever happens with the weather, happens. Whatever happens with the whales, happens. Either way, it doesn't change the fact that my sister kicks butt."

"Thanks." Joey reached down and gave her sister a hug.

"Hang in there, Joe," Bessie said fondly. "Someday the whole world is going to know just how terrific and special Joey Potter really is."

Chapter 10

Joey stared out at the early Sunday morning gloom. Sunday was dawning just like Saturday had: somber and stormy. Rain pelted against the window. The relentless rain was dashing to the ground any autumn leaves that had been left on the trees.

"Joey?"

She turned around to see Bessie standing, minus her crutches, in the doorway of her bedroom. "What are you doing up without your crutches? And where's Alexander?" Joey frowned. "How do you expect your ankle to heal if you—"

"Alexander is sound asleep. As for how I got here, I hopped. Joey, it's okay." Bessie literally hopped to Joey's bed and sat down. "Weather sucks, huh?"

Joey sighed. "To put it mildly. And today's the last

day for the tourist hordes of quaint Capeside to sight multiple Mobies."

"I told you, Joe. There's no point in getting flipped about stuff you can't control."

"I know." Joey came to sit by her sister. "It's just . . . did you ever feel like too much was out of your control, Bessie? Like everything—from world events to the utterly pointless minutiae of your puny, little life—is actually totally out of your hands, and that we're all just pretending that we can control our destinies to make ourselves feel better?"

"I think the rain is getting to you, Joey. But yes, I've had my moments."

"I seem to be having a prolonged moment, Bessie. I don't know what's going on between me and Dawson and Pacey anymore. We act like everything is just so keen and normal. We're some Andy Rooney–Judy Garland-lets-put-on-a-show insipid parody of carefree teendom, when the truth is that everyone is hurt, everyone is suffering, and no one knows what to do about it."

"Give it time, Joey," Bessie advised, hugging her sister's shoulders.

"Right. Time heals all wounds and all that jazz. I'll have to get back to you on that." Joey stood. "Well, time for Judy Garland to make her dramatic entrance into the kitchen and do the breakfast-for-disgruntled-whale-watchers thing. Can I get you anything?"

"I'm cool, Joey," Bessie assured her. "Try not to be so hard on yourself, okay?"

She managed a wry smile. "Okay."

When she got to the kitchen, Joey turned on the coffee maker and mentally ticked off everything that she'd prepared last night with her friends' help—muffins and scones, eight quiches that were in the fridge waiting to be popped into the oven, three kinds of juice, four kinds of fruit yogurt with—

"I believe I've awakened to the vision of an angel," Elvis said from the kitchen doorway.

Just what I need, Joey thought. She mustered up a friendly smile.

"Good morning, Elvis. The coffee is perking."

"I'm feeling pretty danged perky myself, pretty mama." He sashayed across the kitchen toward her.

"I'm really busy now, Elvis—"

"Can I help?"

"Gee, no, thanks, though."

He wasn't more than three inches from her when he began to croon,

"Love me tender, love me true . . ."

"Not to be rude, Elvis, but I have work to do, so—"

"Ya get me hot and bothered, little girl."

Well, you get me annoyed and disgusted, Joey thought. In the mood she was in, she was ready to deck him, she really was. Whale Weekend was a disaster anyway. Why not just add injury to insult?

"Look, Elvis—"

"Morning, Potter, the reinforcements have arrived," Pacey said as he came into the kitchen. Water dripped from his slicker onto the kitchen floor. But Joey was happily surprised to see him. He could help her deal with Elvis. She flew over to him and gave him a huge hug.

"Quite the greeting," Pacey said, eyeing Joey carefully.

"I'm just really glad to see you." She kissed him quickly on the lips, then linked her arm through his and pulled him close. "Well, we have to get to work now, Elvis. Right, Pacey?"

"Right. Work, work, work, that's all we do," Pacey said.

Elvis pointed at her. "Hold on there, Joey. Didn't you tell me you already have a boyfriend? Jim or John, something like that?"

"Jack," Joey said.

"Right, Jack. And this is Pacey. So, you one of those loosey-goosey girls?"

Joey threw her hands in the air. "Right, Elvis. You guessed it. I'm a loosey-goosey girl. That's me. I love 'em, I leave 'em."

Elvis shook his head sadly. "Well, that's a crying shame, sweet thing." He looked at Pacey. "You be careful, now. She's a heartbreaker." He drifted into the dining room.

"Unbelievable," Joey muttered.

"Using me to ward off Elvis-impersonating suitors, Potter?"

"As a matter of fact, yes."

"Well, this is a dark day and I am not referring to the Noah-esque flood out there." Pacey leaned against the counter. "It is the Sunday that will go down in infamy as the day I discovered that you're a loosey-goosey girl."

"I'll be sure to mark it on my calendar. Now, can you set the oven at three-fifty?"

"Sure, Luce." He did it, and held the door open as Joey placed quiches on the wire racks. "And might I add that I did not find pretending to be one of your nearest and dearest entirely loathsome. Kinda brought back memories."

Joey, her back to him, began slicing oranges into sections.

"Funny thing, though. Things happen. Everything changed. Even if you pretend that they haven't."

"Nothing's changed," she insisted.

"Fine. Nothing's changed. I don't mind if you lie to me, Joey. But for God's sake, don't lie to yourself. Not talking about things doesn't make them go away."

Finally, she turned to him. "Is that why you came over early? To talk about the past before—" She looked at her watch. "Six forty-five?"

"It seemed like a reasonable notion at the time."

"It is reasonable, Pacey. It's just . . . it's not the time."

"Will it ever be?"

"I don't know."

He nodded slowly. "We're so *Peyton Place,* aren't we?"

She smiled. "More like a rained-out *Fargo*. So if you came over to help before you so kindly go outside to provide ferry service for my hopefully not-too-hungry breakfast guests, you could put the coffee cups on the table."

"Consider it done."

Pacey helped Joey for the next half-hour, then he put his slicker on again to go man the skiff. Joey just concentrated on her work, trying not to think about anything more complicated than getting the quiches out of the oven when they were done and finding a place where her guests could put their wet umbrellas.

Thinking about anything more than that—like about Pacey or Dawson—could only lead to questions for which she had no answers. On a day like today, that would be running on empty.

Dawson and Joey stood near the coffee maker, watching the breakfast guests wolfing down her quiche. "It's a miracle. I may have found a dish I actually make well," Joey told him.

"Quiche me, you fool," Jack quipped, as he sailed by with a platter of hot rolls. Andie poured coffee refills while Jen was clearing dirty dishes. As for Pacey, he was in the skiff, in the process of picking up Patrick, Candace, and Alexis at Dawson's house.

"So far, so excellent," Dawson told her warmly. "You can cook, Joey, you're just not confident about it."

"It must be my subconscious rebelling against all those years working at the Ice House."

"Well, your quiche is a definite hit."

"I'm just hoping I made enough. I think Ike chowed down an entire one by himself already and the Martinos haven't even—"

"Miss Potter, if I might speak to you?" Mr. Martino stood in the hallway.

"Speak of the devil," Joey muttered to Dawson.

She met him in the hallway. Unfortunately, his wife was there, too, as were their packed suitcases. Joey got a sinking feeling in her stomach, but pasted a smile on her face. "How can I help you?" Mrs. Martino dead-eyed her husband, as if silently ordering him to speak up.

"Have you seen the weather?" Mr. Martino finally asked.

"Yes, sir, I have. I assure you I'm just as disappointed as you are."

"I doubt it. You didn't pay to be here," Mrs. Martino snapped.

"That's true. But as much as I'd like to be powerful enough to have control over the weather, I'm afraid it's just something beyond my control. We here at the B and B are doing our best to provide you with a pleasant weekend in spite of the elements."

Mrs. Martino nodded at her husband. Reluctantly, he pulled a paper from his pants pocket. "Uh, in addition to the weather, there are one or two things that my wife—"

Mrs. Martino cleared her throat ostentatiously.

"That is, that my wife and I have found to be less than satisfactory," Mr. Martino went on.

Uh oh. Not good.

"I'm sorry to hear that, Mr. Martino."

"Oh, well, they aren't really big things," he began, but his wife grabbed the list from her husband.

"Number one. Inadequate food choices at meals. Number two. Zero concern for the health or dietary concerns of the guests. Three. No snacks were provided. Four. No herbal teas. Five. Mattress on bed too soft. Six—"

"I think I get the basic picture of your unhappiness, Mrs. Martino," Joey cut in. "I'm very sorry you weren't happy here. We are fairly new, though, and we're trying to improve."

She eyed Joey disdainfully. "Be that as it may, you aren't charging 'we're still trying to improve' prices, are you? No. Instead, we paid full price for poor quality. We are checking out immediately and I want a refund. In full."

"Can I be of assistance?" Dawson appeared in the doorway.

Joey shook her head, and turned back to Mrs. Martino. "I'm sorry, Mrs. Martino. I'd be happy to refund to you the pro-rated cost of today's breakfast and lunch, since you're checking out before you eat. But our policy is not to offer refunds for time already spent here."

"That's unacceptable," Mrs. Martino insisted.

Dawson walked over to Joey. "Is there some problem here?"

"I can handle this, Dawson," Joey warned, her voice low.

But he was undeterred. "Are you folks unhappy in some way?"

"No, pretty much in every way," Mrs. Martino said. "On top of the poor service, food, and accommodations, we might as well be in the center of a typhoon. I would prefer to ride it out home in New York, in my own bed."

Dawson smiled. "I understand, just as I'm sure you understand that Potter's Bed and Breakfast is a business. I believe we provided every amenity as described, so I'm sure you see that it's unreasonable to ask for a refund at this time."

"It's really very simple. I either get a complete refund or I call the Better Business Bureau first thing Monday morning. Not to mention *certain other people.*"

She means that newspaper writer who's their friend, Joey realized. *That could ruin us.*

"Mrs. Martino, customer satisfaction is our business. And while I go on the record as saying I don't agree with you, I'm certainly willing to make sure that you leave our B and B satisfied, one way or another. I'll bring you a check."

"Just a moment," Dawson said. "Mrs. Martino, don't you agree that it would be more than reasonable for Miss Potter to refund half the amount you paid?"

Mrs. Martino's lip curled into a cold smile. "No."

Joey looked at Mr. Martino. He looked as uncomfortable as he could be. She decided to take a chance. "Mr. Martino," she asked, "do you have the same feelings about this weekend as your wife? Do you want a full refund?"

"No," he said quickly. "I actually was pretty satisfied with—"

"Roland!" his wife exclaimed. "How could you—"

"Mavis, I'm just telling the truth. You don't want me to lie to the young lady, do you? That wouldn't be right."

Mrs. Martino fumed, but the damage had been done. Joey went to the checkbook, but only wrote a refund check for half the cost of the Martinos' weekend. She handed it to Mrs. Martino, who crammed it into her purse.

"Thank you," she said icily. "Be glad you're not going to be my husband for the ride home. And we'll need someone to carry our bags out to the car."

"I can do that," Mr. Martino protested.

"No problem, sir. Happy to help." Dawson picked up their luggage and carried it out, Mr. Martino holding an umbrella over him all the way. By the time they got to their car, Pacey was walking up from the boat dock.

"What's going on?" Pacey asked Joey. He was drenched. "I saw Dawson carrying the Martinos' luggage out."

"The Wicked Witch of the West and her mild-mannered hubby just departed, after a sizeable refund. Evidently my innkeeping skills leave something to be desired."

"Don't take it personally, Potter," Pacey insisted. "It isn't you, it's the crappy weather. Trump Plaza wouldn't look good in rain like this."

"There's no whale-watching at Trump Plaza, Pacey. And I imagine that The Donald manages to make his mortgage payments just fine. Now, where are Patrick, Candace, and Alexis?"

"Don't ask."

Joey groaned. "Why do I feel as if your other Reebok is about to fall?"

"Well . . . Patrick and Candace just caught a cab to Boston. They've checked out."

"But why?" Joey asked wildly.

"Like I told you, the weather. It's not personal."

"But maybe it would have cleared up later and—"

"It's their honeymoon, Joey. They can spend it in

bed anywhere. And that's what they decided to do. In Boston."

"Did Alexis go with them?"

"I'm not sure whether this is good or bad, but no. They released her from service and she stayed. But she said she didn't want to get soaked in the skiff, so she's skipping breakfast." Pacey draped an arm around Joey's shoulders. "Look at it this way, Potter. At least the newlyweds didn't ask for a refund."

"True. But somehow I don't think we can count on them for repeat business, either."

A soaking wet Dawson came to join them. "Mission accomplished. You could have stood your ground, Joey. She was wrong."

"No I couldn't. I have to keep the customers satisfied."

"A Heidi Fleiss moment," Pacey observed.

"Hey, Joey? The Sumo boys just polished off the quiche," Andie called from the kitchen. "Got any more?"

"I made eight!"

"Gone!"

"Offer them some scrambled eggs. But feel free to drop a healthy weight chart somewhere where they can see it," Joey said, as she led Dawson and Pacey back to the kitchen.

Andie was there, already scrambling a dozen eggs in a bowl. "I'll leave that to you, Joey. With the Sumos, I do not mess."

"Mom, are you sure you're up to this?" Dawson asked, as he handed his mother a cup of tea.

"I'm fine, sweetie, really. So is your dad."

It was two hours later. Ms. Gerkin had called an emergency meeting of the Whale Weekend steering committee, to see if there was any possible way to salvage anything from the event. Gale and Mitch had been released from the hospital early that morning, and were at the meeting. In fact, it was being held in their restaurant. As for Dawson and Pacey, they'd simply stopped by to see if they could help in any way.

"As you all know," Ms. Gerkin began, rain pelting hard against the glass storefront of the restaurant, "only a few dozen intrepid souls ventured to the bluffs this morning. They could barely see their hands in front of their faces; they certainly didn't sight any whales."

There were general murmurs of acknowledgment from the three dozen people in the room.

"And, as you also know," Ms. Gerkin continued, "the big Sunday afternoon beach clambake is normally the highlight of Whale Weekend. This year, the beach is a flood zone. Half the tourists are already gone. If there is any possible way to extend some goodwill to the folks who've stuck this out and maybe induce them to come back next year, I certainly am open to ideas. But they'd better come fast."

Mr. Gilette, who owned Pizza-Pizza, raised his hand.

"Yes, Mr. Gilette?"

"What if we give the folks who've stayed vouchers good for next year's weekend? You know, a rain-check?"

"Nice idea, Mr. Gilette," Ms. Gerkin acknowledged. "However, that means that even if they do come back next year, they won't be a revenue source."

"A partial raincheck, then," someone suggested.

Ms. Gerkin nodded. "I'll certainly look into it."

Pacey leaned close to Dawson. "That's Chamber of Commerce-speak for: 'No way, José.' "

Dawson saw his father raise his hand. "I have a proposal," Mitch said, when he was recognized.

"Yes, Mr. Leery?"

"Perhaps we could have the clambake here at the restaurant."

People began to discuss the idea with each other in loud, excited voices. Dawson craned around to look at his mother. "Did he consult you on that one?"

"No," Gale admitted.

"You don't have to, Mom," Dawson said. "You just recovered from food poisoning. Someone else can step up to the plate—no pun intended."

"I know that, Dawson," Gale said. She thought for a moment. "I really do feel fine." Her eyes met Mitch's across the room.

"Gale?" Ms. Gerkin asked. "We all know that you and Mitch were recently ill—"

"So were about a dozen of the people here!" someone called out.

"True," Gale said. She nodded. "I think having the clambake here is a great idea."

"Excellent. Now, if you would all go back to your businesses and spread the word to all our guests that the clambake will take place here, at three o'clock.

And I'm sure Gale and Mitch will take all the help they can get."

"You said it," Mitch agreed.

"Hold up, hold up," Mr. Gilette called, standing up. "Look, I don't want to put a damper on this thing, but everyone knows it's not just a clambake. There's entertainment. Kids dig for colored clams, there's pin-the-tail-on-the-whale, et cetera. What I'm saying is, with all due respect, I don't think people are gonna stick around in this rain just to eat some clams in a restaurant."

"I'd like to propose something," Pacey called, and heads swung in his direction. "What if we were to provide our own entertainment?"

"What entertainment would that be, Mr. Witter?" Ms. Gerkin asked.

"What if I were to promise that it would be unique, fun, exciting, even educational?" Pacey asked.

"What if I were to say 'What drugs are you on, boy'?" Mr. Gilette asked him.

"I am, sir, a man with a plan," Pacey declared, but Mr. Gilette looked doubtful.

"People, people." Gale raised her voice over the rumblings of discontent. "I would just like to say that I know Pacey. And if he says he can provide that kind of entertainment, then he can."

"And I'll help him," Dawson added.

There was a long moment of silence. Then Ms. Gerkin shrugged. "I say, we give it a shot. I don't think there's much choice. Let's get to work."

The crowd dispersed; it seemed like each person heading out into the drenching rain looked toward the skies for a sign of sunshine. There was none. When the last person was gone, Dawson closed the front door of the restaurant and looked at Pacey. "You do have an actual plan in mind, I'm assuming?"

"That would be a correct assumption," Pacey said. Gale and Mitch drifted over, waiting for Pacey to explain.

"We backed you up on this, Pacey, so we're all responsible," Gale told Pacey. "So, what's up?"

Dawson put his hand on Pacey's shoulder. "No pressure, Pace. But just so you realize: if we blow this, we will have put the final nail in the coffin of Weekend of the Whales."

Chapter 11

The restaurant was packed to the gills; the front door was propped open to let air circulate. The clambake cooking itself had actually been done in a pit that had been dug behind the firehouse. In that pit, lobsters, clams, mussels, scallops, corn on the cob, and sweet potatoes had been layered with hot rocks and seaweed, and then baked until it was all perfect. Then, it had been carried to the restaurant literally on the firehouse's emergency stretchers.

Rather than do a buffet table, as would have happened if the clambake had taken place as scheduled on the beach, Mitch and Gale had decided that they would serve individual plates of food to the guests. But the plates would be identical, for simplicity's sake. So the kitchen had been a beehive of activity, as Dawson, Pacey, and their friends loaded food onto plates, than ran those plates out of the kitchen to their guests.

So far, the impromptu clambake was working. People were getting fed. And no one was complaining. That they could get all these people fed at once in the restaurant actually seemed like a small miracle.

Now, all the guests had been served. For a brief moment, Andie stopped rushing from table to table, and she took in the scene of happy, hungry people. The loudest sound in the room was the sound of cracking lobster shells.

"Pretty amazing, huh?" Jen said, coming up next to her.

"That's just what I was thinking. That this got pulled together so quickly seems like some kind of miracle."

Jen smiled. "If Noah could do the Flood, we can do a clam bake."

"Providing Pacey comes through with the entertainment thing." Andie bit anxiously at her lower lip. "He wouldn't tell me what it was."

"Me neither. But if there's one interesting thing I've learned about Pacey," Jen opined, "it's that to underestimate him is usually a major mistake."

"One that happens all the time," Andie said softly. She looked over at Pacey, who stood across the restaurant, engaged in an animated conversation with Alexis, of all people.

"She can't be the entertainment," Andie ventured. "Can she?"

Jen frowned. "Highly doubtful. Girls like Alexis

expect to be the ones entertained." She watched Joey place a new tub of corn on the cob on the side table, then come over to join them.

"This is going better than we had any right to expect. No one brought sandwiches with mayo, did they?"

Jen nodded. "I'm really glad you came, Joey."

"Well, there's no one back at Potter's B and B now except Bessie and Alexander. And Bessie practically forced me out of the house."

"Smart sister," Jen said.

A little boy with red hair and freckles approached Andie. "Hey, are you in charge here? When does the show start?" he asked.

"Soon," Andie promised.

The little boy hitched up his pants. "Are there whales in it?"

"Gee, I don't know," Andie said through her bright smile. "But it's gonna be terrific, I know that much."

He folded his arms. "Not unless I see whales dancing or something."

"Charmer, come over here and let the girls work," his mother called, beckoning the kid back to their table.

He ignored her. "This better be good, or else. I hate the food," he added, then headed back to his mom.

Jen's eyes followed the kid. "His name is *Charmer?*"

"Maybe it was wishful thinking," Joey mused. "Do you think Pacey can come up with dancing whales?"

Andie sighed. "He's good. But he's not that good. Uh oh."

"What?" Jen asked.

Pacey provided the answer to her question, by

banging on a spaghetti pot with a metal spoon. He literally was standing on a table at the far end of the restaurant, his head not more than a foot from the ceiling. In fact, he had pushed three or four tables together to create a makeshift stage.

"Ladies and gentlemen, if I might have your attention," Pacey called through cupped hands, since the restaurant lacked a mike. "I'm Pacey Witter, your M.C. for Whale Weekend's Whale of a Show. How about this beach we're on? Everyone enjoying it?"

"No," Charmer yelled, and people laughed good-naturedly.

"Easy kid, you don't want to end up as whale bait. Anyway, everyone, welcome to Capeside," Pacey told the crowd. "Sorry about the weather, we called the White House last week, and they promised that it would be nice. But we're not gonna let it rain out the fun, folks. Right?"

The room was silent.

"Not promising," Jen whispered to Andie.

"Right! Well, we've got a lot of surprises for you," Pacey went on, slightly less confident now. "To open our show, our very own Whale Weekend coordinator, Lydia Gerkin, will sing for us. Let's give it up for Lydia!"

Pacey clapped enthusiastically, hoping to get the restaurant excited. But very few people joined in the clapping as Ms. Gerkin climbed up on the table with an acoustic guitar.

"Hello, nice people," Ms. Gerkin trilled. "This is an original song called 'From Sea to Shining Sea.' "

Ms. Gerkin sang in a pleasant, thin voice. It was a story song about a fisherman lost at sea. It went on.

And on.

And on.

At first, the crowd listened politely. Then, people started to fidget in their seats—the restaurant was jammed with people and the air was getting stuffy. Then, conversations started all over the restaurant, as the song showed no signs of coming to a conclusion.

Andie edged over to where Jonathan and Michael White were sitting together, and leaned down near Michael's ear. "How many verses of that thing can there possibly be?" she groaned. "Can't she just sink the whaling ship and end it already?"

Finally, after what felt like an eternity, Ms. Gerkin brought her song to a close. Pacey applauded as if she'd just won an Oscar, and three or four kind people joined in.

"Thank you, Ms. Gerkin," Pacey said. "That was . . . inspirational."

Michael leaned toward Andie. "Yeah. It could inspire a mass exodus."

"Okay, moving right along. Now for something really terrific," Pacey said, sounding like a stand-up comic who knew his act was dying. "You've never seen anything like this before, and I guarantee you'll never see anything like them again. Put your hands together for the improv slam poetry of The Sumo Brothers!"

A few people applauded; most watched, gape-mouthed, as the four enormous poets clambered up on the tables. They were so tall that their heads nearly scraped the ceiling, so wide that Mike and

Ike, standing on the outside, were dangerously close to falling down.

Fred folded his arms and waited for the crowd to quiet completely. "Hey, people. I'm Fred. That's Ike, Mike, and Elvis. We're poets. Tonight, in honor of Weekend of the Whales and the good people of Capeside, we're gonna do something a little different: improv slam poetry with a nautical theme. Can you give us a few words that have to do with the sea? Just call 'em out."

The crowd was silent. "Come on, people," Pacey exhorted from the sidelines. "Give 'em some ideas."

Finally, a few ideas were called out half-heartedly. "Free Willy!"

"Drowning!"

"Moby Dick?"

"Oil slicks!"

Fred made a comic face. "Moby Dick? Free Willy? Is that the best you can come up with? Okay, Moby Dick and Free Willy it is. The words were Free Willy, drowning, Moby Dick, and oil slicks. Ready, boys?"

The Sumos nodded vigorously. Ike started to make percussion sounds with his lips; the other three joined in by smacking their huge torsos with their hands in various places, almost as if they were organic tympani.

"Put 'em in *Stomp*," Jonathan suggested to his brother and Andie, half-joking. But it didn't take long until the Sumos had a serious hip-hop groove underway. Then, as if they'd rehearsed it a thousand times, Ike stepped forward as the other three stepped back, and started to speak in rhyme.

The day I saw Free Willy, that whale wasn't silly
He swam and he spouted all willy-nilly.

He motioned to the other Sumos; Mike jumped forward, and took over without missing a beat.

I thought he was drowning and started up frowning
But a whale is a mammal, stores air like a camel.

Unprompted this time, Fred stepped up to join Mike.

Now this whale of a tale, it just can't fail
'Cuz whales can swim like a ship can sail.

And finally, it was Elvis's turn to join the other three.

My big concern was this oil slick
I'm thinking Willy's sinking, gonna get all sick
With the goo and the muck if he sucks it up
So I cleaned up the spill so Willy can chill
And the oil in the water won't get her ill
Yes Willie's Wilhelmina; ain't that slick?
When she got freed she went and married Moby Dick!

The reaction in the restaurant was instantaneous—people were applauding like crazy, laughing and whooping in reaction to the improvised poem. Jen nudged Joey in the arm. "Maybe you should have gone for Elvis after all," she teased. "He's great!"

Joey was in a state of shock. "I believe this is one of those proverbial 'can't judge a book by its cover' moments."

By this time, the crowd was yelling for an encore. And, for the next half-hour, the Sumo brothers both improvised poetry for the crowd and did some prepared pieces. Elvis even delivered some material from *Moby Dick* by memory, but reciting it as if it were poetry. That was what finally brought the crowd to its feet, rising as one in a standing ovation.

As Dawson applauded as hard as anyone, two slender arms snaked their way around him from behind. Alexis. Joey and Jen traded looks—they'd had enough of the young videographer. To their mutual shock, Dawson smiled at the girl. "How terrific was that?" he asked.

"Decent," she said. "You know, now that I'm freed from the shackles of honeymoon videoing, I'm actually having fun." She hugged him, then hurried off, as if she had somewhere to go.

"How low the mighty have fallen," Jen chided him.

"I can't believe you actually fell for her rich, preppie, snotty, the-world-revolves-around-wonderful-me smarm," Joey sputtered. "Dawson, not that I would dream of influencing your feelings on the subject, but she is—in a word—loathsome."

Dawson just smiled.

"You know, I saw this in *Invasion of the Body Snatchers,*" Jen told Joey. "It looks like Dawson, and it walks like Dawson—"

Up on stage, Pacey got the audience's attention, as

Mr. Gilette and three other guys wheeled in a big-screen TV.

"You know," Pacey began, "the truly brave and truly crazy amongst you went out on the *Capeside Queen* to look for whales. And see whales they did. Unfortunately, the rest of us landlubbers didn't get to share in the experience. But some awesome footage was shot on that vessel, that we've put together with some other video taken by our own Dawson Leery when the Capeside beach was at its sunny best."

Someone dimmed the lights in the restaurant and illuminated the television. There, in all its glory, was the view from Dunn's Lighthouse on an absolutely gorgeous fall day, with the setting sun to the west.

Pacey continued as the video unspooled. "While you watch the film," he announced, "we have a real treat to share with you. One of the foremost oceanographers in the world is in Capeside for Whale Weekend, and she has agreed to talk to us about the magical world of the whales that so few of us know. She's amazing. Please welcome Dr. Dorothy White."

People applauded as Dr. White went and stood by the big-screen TV, which was now showing Alexis's video of the *Capeside Queen* departing the marina the day before.

"Did you guys know about this?" Andie asked Michael and Jonathan.

"Frankly, no," Michael admitted.

Dr. White's voice boomed out through the crowd. "Beluga. Blue. Bottlenose. Humpback, Orca. Sperm. Killer. What do these words have in common? They are all types of the magical mammals known to us as whales. Let there be no doubt: not only are whales intelligent, they are perhaps more intelligent than we are. They speak. They sing, they play."

The TV video now showed a seasick Dawson, huddled in the cabin of the *Capeside Queen*, as the camera rocked up and down with the violent ocean swells.

"And, to their credit, they never get seasick," Dr. White continued, as everyone laughed. "Did you know that the blue whale is bigger than any of the dinosaurs were?"

"Wow," Charmer breathed, loud enough for Dr. White to hear. "That's big."

"Yes, young man," Dr. White said, "That's very big. Over one hundred feet long—the size of a nine-story building—at weights of more than one hundred and fifty tons. Sumo boys, you're puny in comparison, despite your obvious talents."

The crowded restaurant laughed uproariously. On the video screen, the camera panned the ocean, then zeroed in on the Sumo brothers, fishing for their dinner.

"And what of the infamous Moby Dick, whom the brothers used so cleverly in their improvised poem? Moby Dick was a sperm whale, a mystery to this day. In their forehead there is a huge reservoir of clear oil, and we still are not certain why. Nor do we know why this animal has a twenty pound brain—the largest brain of any animal that ever lived."

Joey leaned toward Jen. "I've lived in Capeside my entire life and I didn't know any of this," she mur-

mured. Suddenly, on the TV screen, two humpback whales breached in the water, a couple of hundred yards from the *Capeside Queen.* People audibly gasped at the sight.

"These are humpback whales," Dr. White continued, "the type of whale seen most commonly off the coast of Capeside."

Suddenly, the water was churning with the whales; people watching just what Dawson had seen on his voyage the day before on the *Capeside Queen.* As he watched it anew, his seasickness was long forgotten.

"Here we have an entire pod—or group—of humpbacks. They come in four different colors, and sing the most amazing songs."

Dr. White narrated the entire *Capeside Queen* segment of the video. And then, as it finished, the pictures changed to some that Dawson had shot from Pacey's sailboat over the summer, and then, to the same view that opened the show, from Dunn's Lighthouse in the autumn.

"You know, Joey, sometimes I forget how truly beautiful it is here," Jen whispered.

"I know just what you mean," Joey said.

"In the future, let's try to remind each other to stop the self-involved teen angst now and then and really *see* it. What do you think?"

"I think," Joey said, extending her hand, "you have yourself a deal."

Chapter 12

A few hours later, Dr. White and her nephews stood on the porch of Grams's house, luggage at their feet. Grams, Jen, and Andie stood with them.

"I hope you enjoyed your trip to Capeside in spite of the weather," Grams told them. "Ironic, isn't it? The rain seems to have stopped."

Dr. White smiled. "I have to confess, I was more than skeptical when I decided to talk my nephews into this, but the truth is, I think we all had a wonderful time." She and Grams hugged warmly. "And I feel as if I've found a new friend, too."

From the light in Grams's eyes, she clearly agreed. "Next time you come for a visit, we'll do something even more wild," she promised.

Jen looked at her thoughtfully. "You never did tell me what mischief you two got into last night."

"Jennifer, dear, I never will."

"My grandmother has been known to lead many a good woman astray with her wild ways," Jonathan teased.

"And you, young man, can only hope that you inherited my sense of adventure," Professor White told him.

Michael tugged on Andie's hand. She gave him a questioning look and then realized he couldn't see it. But maybe he could sense it. "There's something I wanted to show you," he said.

"What?"

"In the backyard."

Andie shrugged. "Okay. Excuse us." Hand in hand, she led him to the rear of the house. "Just let me know if this is incredibly crass or insensitive, Michael, but how can you show me something you can't see?"

Michael laughed. "You see, that's one of the things I like about you, Andie. You just come right out and say things. You're not afraid to ask questions, and you don't treat me as if I'm mentally deficient just because I'm blind."

"Well, aren't I nice," she teased.

"Yeah. More than." He reached for her other hand, then slowly leaned forward and softly kissed her forehead.

"Amazing," Andie said. "How did you know exactly where my forehead was?"

"Andie?"

"Yuh?"

"You know that thing I said I wanted to show you?"

"Yuh."

"This is it." This time he took her into his arms and kissed her for real. At first, it caught her by surprise. But before she had time to consider how she felt, she found herself kissing him back. Finally, he broke away. "I definitely liked that."

"I definitely did, too," she admitted. "But I still don't know how you—"

"Think about it, Andie. When you go to kiss a guy, don't you close your eyes first?"

She thought about it. "You know, you're right."

"So you see," Michael said, "when it comes to love, we're all in the dark. I had a truly terrific weekend, Andie. It was a blast." He gave her a quick hug, and patted the back pocket of his jeans. "I have your phone number right here in my wallet."

"Don't tell me, you have a voice-activated phone dialer."

"Let me ask you this. If I didn't call you, would you call me?"

"Honestly, Michael, I'm not sure."

He exhaled slowly. "That wasn't necessarily the answer I was hoping for."

"Well, it's just honest Andie and her honest answers. I really do like you. And I'd like to get to know you better. And I'm definitely attracted to you—"

"I sense a 'but' coming up real soon," Michael interjected.

"But. My romantic life has gotten kind of complicated. And I need to figure a few things out before I jump into anything else."

Michael touched her arm. "Got it. Well, I hope

you untangle your entanglements. But in the meantime, I would really like to be your friend."

She put her hands on her hips. "Is this one of those things where you're saying you want us to be friends when what you really mean is that you're hoping that if we're together we'll just spontaneously become more than friends and end up naked on a bearskin rug overcome with passion?"

He laughed. "I like the way your mind works."

"Just checking."

They shared one more tender kiss. Then Andie took his hand and led him back to the porch.

"You ready to take off, bro?" Jonathan asked. "Dorothy's already in the car, waiting for us."

"Ready as I'm gonna get," Michael said.

Jonathan took in their entwined hands. "I still say you picked the dweebier brother, Andie."

"Yeah, yeah, you just can't take the comp," Michael taunted playfully.

Once again, it struck Andie how close they were. It warmed her heart. "I hope the two of you realize how lucky you are to have each other."

"This Bozo?" Michael scoffed.

"Yeah," Andie said softly. "That Bozo."

"Trust me on this, Andie," Jonathan said. "I'm the lucky one. Catch you around."

Michael took Jonathan's arm. They descended the porch steps together and got into their grandmother's car. As it pulled away, Jen joined Andie. "Nice guys, huh?" Jen said.

Andie nodded. "Ever wish you had a sister or a brother, Jen?"

"Well, I used to always say that I loved being an only child because no one else ran up my parents' credit card. But these days, truthfully? Yeah. You're lucky to have Jack, you know."

"Funny. That's what I just told Michael and Jonathan about each other. And I was just thinking the exact same thing about me and Jack."

Gale, Mitch, and Dawson sat at an empty table, their sore feet propped up on chairs. "What do you think, Dawson?" Gale asked. "I'd say our indoor clambake—on zero notice—was something of a success."

"Without a doubt," Dawson agreed. He looked from one parent to the other. "Has anyone ever mentioned how well you two work together?

"It was so patently obvious to everyone who knows you that you were meant to be together. I'm glad you finally figured it out. Knowing you have each other will make it easier for me when I eventually go away to college."

"Forget it, we're not letting you graduate," Mitch groaned. "I cannot possibly have a son who is that old."

"I just don't want the two of you to look back and regret the time that you lost," Dawson said softly, "when you could have been together. Anyway, I have to go. I'm meeting everyone at Joey's. We're going out to the lighthouse for a postmortem."

Just as Dawson was about to walk out the door, his father called to him. "Son?"

Dawson turned.

"I'm glad your Mom and I finally figured it out too." Mitch smiled. "Give Joey our regards."

"You realize you suck, Potter," Pacey told her, as they carefully made their way across the wood-covered trail that led out to Dunn's Lighthouse. Behind them, Jack, Jen, Dawson, and Andie followed in a single file.

The late afternoon was brightening, as thin gray coils of clouds scudded across a sky that was deep blue to the west. And the air was turning chilly; a cold front definitely was coming through. Not soon enough to save Whale Weekend, though. Just about every tourist had left town right after the clambake.

"Would you care to explain that statement?" Joey responded.

"Face it, Joey," Pacey went on. "The Sumo brothers basically saved our butts, and you refused to kiss Elvis good-bye."

"Sorry, Pacey, I don't believe in 'thank you' tongue."

Jack made a face. "I heard that. That's disgusting."

"Evidently Dawson's a believer." Jen teased. "I saw him with Miss Tall, Dark, and Stylishly Anorexic before she left. Isn't that true, Dawson?"

"I may have reluctantly shared an assuredly non-passionate, very short-lived exchange of above-the-neck facial contact with Alexis," Dawson said. "Though I did not instigate it. And it was not, as you so quaintly put it, 'mercy tongue.' "

"Hey, ease up on Dawson," Pacey reminded them.

"Alexis was the one with the videotape from the *Capeside Queen.* No videotape, no TV show at the clambake. No TV show at the clambake, there might have been a riot in downtown Capeside. Consider what Dawson did as his civic duty."

"I don't think so," Jen commented.

Pacey grinned, and helped Joey over a place where the wood path had sunk down into the muck. "Okay. But at least people got to see that there really were whales out there."

Joey gingerly stepped past the sunken planks. "Well, if it rains for next year's Weekend of the Whales, I am not repeating this year's fiasco. I don't care if Bessie is in traction. Remind me that I said as much, please."

"But the fact is, except for the refund to the Psycho Childrens' Television Producer from Hell, you cleaned up," Pacey reminded her. "All that money socked away to pay your mortgage."

They walked in silence for several minutes, until they came to the base of the lighthouse. The sky continued to brighten, even though there was not more than thirty or forty minutes of daylight left before sunset.

"It's true that things worked out reasonably well," Joey said softly. "And it's true that I didn't have Bessie or Bodie's help. And we all know I massively stressed over it. But then all of you . . . what you did for me . . ."

The rest of her sentence trailed off.

"I believe that, in her own inarticulate way, Ms. Potter is attempting to thank us," Jen said.

"I *am* thanking you," Joey said firmly. "I never, ever, could have done this without you. All of you. I mean, you guys basically gave up your entire weekend. You got up early and stayed up late and put up with so much crap just to help me."

Pacey shrugged. "Yeah, and we got soaked too. So what's your point?"

"My point is, I think I have reached the outer limits of my smarm quota," Joey said. "I trust you all can fill in any blank spots in my diabetes-inducing diatribe."

"Fine," Andie said. "Race ya up!" Without waiting, she ran to the back of the lighthouse, opened the door, and charged up the stairs. Up, up, up they all ran, until, breathless, they reached the top.

An incredible vista awaited them. The sky was now almost completely blue, the ocean the same color as the sky; it was impossible to see where the ocean ended and the sky began.

"I see nature is playing a cruel and mercurial trick on the village of Capeside," Pacey said, breathing hard. "Why couldn't this have happened three hours ago?"

They looked out at the vast ocean. "When I saw the video from the *Capeside Queen,* dark and gloomy and seasick-inducing as the trip looked, I felt envious," Jen said softly. "I've never seen a whale."

"It's roughly Elvis, with a spout," Pacey said.

Joey looked dreamily down at the ocean. "When Bessie and I were kids, my parents used to take us out here, and we'd sit on the cliffs. This was before anyone invented Weekend of the Whales. We'd wait so quietly for the magic to begin. And it always did—all those massive, beautiful creatures, putting on a show just for us. It made my mom laugh, and my dad would pick her up and whirl her around in a circle. We were so happy."

Dawson remembered. He'd been on one of these excursions with the Potters, back before her mom's death, back before her dad went to jail. Joey had survived it all, amazingly. And she continued to survive. Sometimes, even, to thrive.

He studied her profile. It was indescribably beautiful to him—he knew it as well as he knew his own. Maybe better. She was his Joey. How could she ever be anything else?

"Look!" Andie cried, pointing east, a few hundred yards out. The water was alive. Three humpback whales had their heads up out of the water. And for all the world, it looked like they were looking directly at the lighthouse.

"I never saw them this close," Joey marveled. "Oh God, they're so beautiful."

As if on cue, the three whales ducked under the water, and then breached in unison. The smack of their huge fin-splayed bodies against the ocean surface could be heard all the way to the top of the lighthouse.

"This is great!" Jen's eyes shined. "Everyone in the whole world should get to see this at least once."

"I agree," Jack said with awe, as the whales breached again. "Amazing."

Joey turned to Dawson and Pacey. "We'll miss this, won't we? When we all go away to college, I mean."

"I'm thinking, we all just keep flunking senior year

and kind of slow down life's little minuet, whaddaya think?" Pacey suggested.

" 'Time waits for no man,' " Dawson quoted.

"Yeah," Andie agreed. "Shakespeare said that. And he's dead."

Joey's lips curled into a smile. "But we're not. And they're not." The pod of whales flew into the air again, as if jumping with the simple joy of being alive.

Andie went to the open edge of the lighthouse. "Call me Ishmael!" she shouted into the sea breeze. "No. Call us Ishmael! No. Call us a pod of Ishmaels!"

"McPhee," Pacey said, "sometimes I wonder about you."

But they all knew what Andie had meant. Deep down, they even knew it was true. And they wouldn't have had it any other way.

About the Author

C. J. Anders is a pseudonym for a well-known young adult fiction–writing couple.

Dawson's Creek Collection

Dawson's Creek novels are available to collect in three omnibus editions.

Dawson's Creek: Omnibus 1

The Beginning of Everything Else

Shifting Into Overdrive

Long Hot Summer

Dawson's Creek: Omnibus 2

Calm Before The Storm

Double Exposure

Major Meltdown

Dawson's Creek: Omnibus 3

Trouble In Paradise

Too Hot To Handle

Don't Scream